UNDEAD MAGIC

THE WITCH IN HURTLER'S GULCH

WENDY MEADOWS

Majestic Owl Publishing LLC
P.O. Box 997
Newport, NH 03773

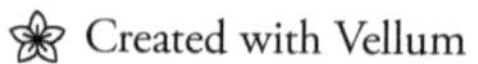 Created with Vellum

CHAPTER ONE

A ghostly cloud of silver vapor swirled in a surreal shape before forming the distinct image of a female face. Her lips parted in a glorious smile and then, without warning, a deafening explosion erupted, blasting the apparition to nothing. An almighty smash shot yellow-orange flames in all directions and the shockwave shattered all the windows on every side.

For one long, terrible moment, darkness descended and obliterated all else.

All at once, someone switched on the lights and everyone sitting in the circle turned as one to stare at little old me.

Directly across from me, tall, terrible Samantha Vance raised her bony arm and aimed a crooked, accusing finger at me. "She did it! That wretched, horrid excuse for a witch Katriona Beaty ruined our séance—AGAIN!"

A lump stuck in my throat and I shrank before all those harsh, glaring eyes. "I…I didn't!" I squeaked. "It wasn't me. I didn't do anything."

"Admit it!" Samantha shrieked. "Admit, for once in your life, that you're a complete failure as a witch. Every time we even come close to conjuring our founding ancestor and patron

Varilla Gouch, YOU come along and blow up the house —AGAIN!"

I opened my mouth, but she cut me off with another bellow of outrage. "Look at this place! You destroyed the whole house! How bad does it have to get before you realize you're hopeless? You're not a witch! Do you hear me? You're no witch! You're a blunderer! You're a blister! You're a boil on the buttocks of magic!"

I cowered before the assault, but inspiration failed me— kinda like everything she was saying. No argument strong enough came to my mind to counter her accusations. Okay, so I didn't exactly destroy the *whole* house. I just broke the windows…all of them. Somehow I didn't think saying that would appease Samantha one bit.

In answer to my thoughts, a chill wind whistled through the cavernous remains of the windows, raking the jagged shards of broken glass still clinging to the frames. It cut through my clothes and made my skin crawl…or was that from the glares of my supposed coven sisters?

I scanned their faces one after another. Just a few moments ago, I might have been tempted to call these women my closest friends. Now I wasn't so sure.

"You botched the Smithersley Incantation again, didn't you?" minced scrawny, skeletal Amaya Richards.

"No!" I exclaimed. "I'm sure I didn't."

"You always botch the Smithersley," groused bulging, pompous Eva Mortenson. "You'll never get it right, which means *we'll* never complete the summons with YOU around."

"She's out," Samantha barked. "She doesn't belong here."

"What!" I shrieked. "You're getting rid of me?"

"You're incompetent," she snarled. "You're incapable of learning the most basic spells, much less the more complicated ones we need for our work."

"I'll get better! I'll learn! You can't just throw me out."

Samantha's lip curled upward from her beastly, pointed

teeth. "This is a coven, not a kindergarten. Go learn and get better somewhere else. You don't belong here."

"You…you can't do this!" My gaze darted around the circle searching for someone, anyone, who could help me. "You can't just throw me out. I've been part of this coven for seven years. I've given everything to be a part of it."

Samantha drew herself up and got to her feet. She towered over me and looked down her long nose in my direction. Her upper lip quivered in a revolting kind of way. "This coven will only reconvene when THAT is gone."

She leveled one last devastating finger at me. Then she turned on her heel and stalked out of the room. One after the other, the others got to their feet from the ornate Oriental carpet where we had been kneeling for the séance.

One by one, they followed Samantha away, casting backward glances in my direction, some sneering, some disgusted, some sympathetic, some questioning. In the end, though, they all went—except one.

I looked in despair at Ruby Gleason. She gathered up the cushions and piled them next to their usual cabinet before she migrated to my side. "I'm really sorry, Katriona. I wish there was something I could do. I feel for you. I really do."

I rounded on her in a frenzy. "You can't throw me out, Ruby! It's unheard of! It's against our whole charter. Membership is supposed to be for life after a witch passes all the initiation rites. You know that. You can't do this! You can't throw me out of the coven. This coven is my whole life!"

She shook her head. "I'm really sorry, but you have to go. You know what Samantha's like. Her grandmother is the Grand High Matron of the whole Western Magical Convergence. The others have to follow her lead even if they don't agree with her— which they do—and I have to do the same thing. You have to go. I'm sorry."

I searched her face and then this room in which I'd spent so much of my life these last seven years. That only brought me face to face with those horrible, toothlike windows. They bared their jagged teeth at me exactly like Samantha did. "You can't just…just throw me out on the street for one tiny little mistake. You can't!"

Ruby brought her eyes around to regard me. "It isn't just one tiny little mistake, though, is it, Katriona? This is the fifth time you've screwed up the Smithersley Incantation and you've flubbed other spells, too, with equally disastrous results."

"No, I didn't!" I yelled. "I didn't screw it up! I know I didn't!"

She paused, studying me. "If that's true, perform the Smithersley right now. Go on. Show me how you did it. I'll watch and make sure you can really do it."

I pulled my head in real quick. Now that she challenged me to do it, I wasn't so sure anymore that I *hadn't* screwed it up. I bowed my head and shut my eyes. I concentrated as hard as I could and raised my hand.

I summoned all my power and started to draw shapes in the air with my forefinger. I went through the whole sequence until I felt a stream of energy flowing down my arm, pouring from my hand.

I dared to open my eyes and saw a wisp of cold gray vapor coming out of my finger. It started to pull together into a shape. I drew faster until, without warning, the vapor imploded into a pea-sized ball and popped in a miniature version of the first explosion.

Ruby shook her head again. She had already started to turn away. "I was watching you earlier, too, Katriona, when it happened. You inscribed the pentagram to the lower left point instead of the lower right. It was the same mistake you made the last three times and now look at this place. It's a wreck."

"You can't do this to me! I'll…I'll get better. I'll practice. I'll improve. Isn't that what initiation is supposed to be—learning to get better?"

"You're not an initiate anymore, Katriona," she breathed.

"Anyway, none of us can afford to piss off Samantha. You have to go. I suggest you leave town. If you stick around, she'll only continue to harass you."

"But…" I squeaked. "Where will I go? I have nowhere else to go."

"I'm sorry. I really wish there was something I could do."

She walked out of the room. Now I really was completely, utterly alone—and not just in this room. Everyone I knew in the world, everyone in the world I thought cared about me, was in the next room gathered around that witch Samantha.

She really was a witch. That meant I was just…what—human? All this time I'd spent—days, weeks, years—training in magic. I'd shunned the rest of humanity to dedicate myself to this coven and this was how they repaid me.

Even as I thought that, a nagging voice in the back of my mind whispered, *You deserve it. You're a failure as a witch. You're not a witch. You're a blister. You're a boil on the buttocks of magic.*

Slowly, painfully, I hauled myself to my feet. I didn't want to leave, but I didn't want to stay, either. I crossed the living room to the front door and collected my handbag from the pile under the hall table. I looped it over my shoulder.

Before I walked out the door, I cast a long glance over the house I had considered my true spiritual home. No doubt remained in my mind that I was seeing it for the last time.

My vision swam with the sting of tears. I couldn't let them fall. I couldn't stoop to crying over these venomous women. If they didn't want me because of one mistake, then they weren't worth my tears.

I shook them out of my eyes, swallowed the lump in my throat, and marched through the door. I shut the door behind me and hurried away.

CHAPTER TWO

The barista set my drink down in front of me on the table. "Here you go. Have a great day."

I took one look at the steaming cup and opened my mouth to call her back, but she was already gone. She vanished into the kitchen and left the front counter of the coffee shop unmanned—or unwomaned, as the case may be.

I returned to studying my cup. I ordered white hot chocolate, but the liquid in front of me looked curiously brown. Maybe, just maybe…

I cast one hesitant peek around the coffee shop. The few other patrons all appeared to be occupied with their own drinks. An old lady read a book in the corner—an actual book with pages. How long had it been since I'd seen that? She didn't even have a cell phone within reach. Maybe she was too old to know how to work one.

A young mother by the front window bent over a stroller and spooned whipped cream into her chubby son's mouth. The kid waved his arms and gurgled, spitting cream all over his clothes while he struggled to escape his safety harness. Poor kid.

The third patron, a man in a canvas Carhartt jacket and scuffed jeans and work boots, punched his thumb into the screen of his phone. None of them would notice if I did a little switcheroo. I couldn't possibly be as inept at magic as Samantha implied.

With one last check that the other patrons weren't watching, I pretended to rest my elbows on the table. I picked up a spoon in my left hand and held it poised over the mug while I circled my right forefinger over the cup. Just a quick spell and I could change it to white chocolate. Easy-peasy, right?

The milk on the brown surface swirled by itself and started to spread. It formed a spiral, widening to turn the brown to white when, in a flash, the hot chocolate rocketed out of the cup. A giant brown geyser blasted in all directions. The cup exploded and all the chocolate milk showered over me. It splashed in my face and drenched my clothes.

I sprang back with a startled shriek, but it was too late. Everyone in the coffee shop turned around to stare at me. Stunned and breathless, I dropped my gaze to the disaster. Chocolate milk saturated the tablecloth and that was saying nothing about me. The cooling, sticky liquid dripped from my hair and dribbled down my nose.

Just then, a deep, gruff laugh burst through the pregnant silence. I looked up to see the Carhartt man busting his ribs laughing at me. His blue eyes twinkled and gleamed above the rough whiskers covering his cheeks.

He couldn't know. He couldn't know I blew up my hot chocolate with magic, but his eyes said otherwise. For a second, I half-suspected he knew exactly what I had done going all the way back to that fateful night when Samantha drove me out of the coven. He laughed like he knew exactly how much of a failure I really was.

The barista hustled over at that moment and cut off my view of the guy. She bent over the table patting everything with a towel, including me. "Oh my gosh! I am so sorry. I don't know how this happened."

I couldn't see the guy behind her, but I imagined him

busting a gut over this, too. *He* knew how it happened. He knew only too well, but how?

She mopped up the whole mess, gushing about how much the coffee shop regretted the unfortunate incident, the whole time looking a little confused as to what exactly had happened. She promised to comp my drink and replace it. She even promised to get my clothes dry-cleaned.

"You don't have to do that," I muttered. "I'm fine."

She raced away to the kitchen and came back with another hot chocolate—also brown. In her absence, I saw that the guy had left. So much the better.

She put the cup down and, after another flurry of apologies, left me to my ruminations. I bent over the drink, too grateful that no one had called me out for using magic—or trying to anyway—to care anymore if it was brown or white.

So Samantha was right. I was a failure as a witch. What kind of witch couldn't even turn hot chocolate from brown to white? I wasn't a witch at all. I was nothing but a blister.

I didn't belong in the coven. They were right to throw me out. That was how I wound up here. Hurtler's Gulch. Even the name sounded like I came here to jump off a bridge.

I used my life savings—which wasn't much, come to think of it—to get as far away from Mount Freeman as possible. Now I was here, in this suppurating ulcer of a town, with barely enough money to buy a cup of hot chocolate. I was lucky the barista replaced the one I destroyed because I wouldn't have been able to buy another one.

If the town was a suppurating ulcer and I was a blister, then it must be fate, right? When I looked through the front window at the low, slumped houses and moss-ridden storefronts, I hated this town. It was a match made in heaven, and now I'd made the most stellar entrance imaginable.

I bent over my cup again and dumped in a package of sugar just for good measure. If I was going to rot in this backwater cesspool, I might as well get a head start on sabotaging myself.

I groused under my breath while I stirred it in. "*This is a coven, not a kindergarten.*" How dare she!

Still, maybe she had a little bit of a point. I did screw up quite a few times—okay, a lot of times—but that was no reason to give me the boot. They could at least have given me some coaching. Isn't that what normal people do?

I took a gulp of the hot chocolate only to find it was now sickeningly sweet. I decided to spite myself by not finishing it. I gathered my handbag and extended the handle on the wheeling suitcase I brought with me on the bus. All the earthly possessions I had in the world were inside it.

I wheeled it outside wishing like anything for a shower and a comfortable place to sit down. Now came the hard part: finding a place to stay in this strange town.

The minute I got outside, I confronted the obvious problem. Houses and businesses lined Main Street. I didn't see a library, post office, or anywhere else where I might find any classified ads for rooms for rent.

I trundled my suitcase down the sidewalk searching the town with a sinking heart. Hurtler's Gulch. That bridge was looking real good about now. I got as far as the grocery store and sat down to rest on a random bench. Turned out it was the lone bench in front of the only bus stop in town—the bus stop where yours truly arrived to seize her glorified destiny.

I slid the suitcase handle down into the suitcase and took out my phone. I punched up my web browser and entered *Hurtler's Gulch classified ads* into the search window.

Nothing. Not one listing came up for Hurtler's Gulch. I frowned at the device, trying to understand what in the heck was wrong with it. I checked the indicator in the corner. Yes, I had three bars of cell reception. I flipped over to my email. I definitely had a working internet connection.

On an impulse, I navigated over to Google Maps and tapped in *Hurtler's Gulch* and waited. *No such listing. Please try again.*

I blinked down at it in astonishment. Then I glanced up and

down Main Street. Was I dreaming I was really *in* this pit of a town? According to the internet, this place didn't exist, and everybody knows the internet never lies.

The houses, the people walking up and down, the stores, and even that sticky feeling clinging to my skin—they all seemed real enough. How could a town exist without showing up on the internet? Technically, that shouldn't be possible.

I frowned to my right and left once again. My hand holding the phone fell onto my lap. I struggled to come up with…well, something, some coherent thought to explain this.

Just then, a young woman came striding down the sidewalk. Her glossy black hair swept in glorious waves when she moved and her black eyes glistened.

She angled in and sat down on the bench next to me. She started rummaging in her purse for something and muttering under her breath. "Just when you think you understand someone, they have to go and do something like this. I swear to God, if I wasn't standing right there, I wouldn't have believed it. I mean, is it asking too much to expect a certain degree of human consideration from someone you've been living with for three years?"

I did my best to act like I couldn't hear her. I couldn't believe she was talking to me, but in a heartbeat, she looked up from her open handbag, looked right at me, and went on as though we'd been in the middle of a heartfelt conversation. "I just put my bagel out on the kitchen counter and I got a phone call before I had a chance to put cream cheese on it. I went into my room to get my dad the information he wanted, and when I came back, that cow had cream cheese spread over MY bagel and half of it stuffed into her fat gob. Can you believe that?"

I blinked at her with my mouth open. "Wow. That's nerve for you."

"You ain't lying!" She bowed over her handbag. "So that was the magnificent start to my morning. Now I can't find my stinking, filthy, godawful…Oh, here it is."

She withdrew a compact mirror from her bag, flipped it open, and surveyed her face in the glass for two seconds before she clipped it shut and pitched it back into the bag. She chucked the bag on the bench next to her and rounded on me with flashing eyes. "You're new in town, aren't you?"

I cringed. "Yeah. Sadly."

She snorted with laughter. "You don't know the half of it, sister. What did you do—get released from jail or something? Couldn't you come up with a better destination than this dump?"

I made a face and looked away. "Let's say I did and skip the gory details."

This time, she laughed outright and slapped her knuckles against my arm. "I like you! You've got a sense of humor, which is a lot more than I can say for certain people, if you know what I mean. What's your name?"

"Katriona. Katriona Beaty."

"I'm Jada—Jada Hooper." She stuck out her hand and gave mine a hearty shake. "It's a pleasure to meet a kindred spirit."

I eyed her closer. She was being awfully friendly for someone who didn't know me from a hole in the ground. "How long have you lived here?"

"Who—me?"

"No, the other girl sitting next to you," I fired back. "Who did you think I was talking to?"

She burst out laughing again. "You kill me! Naw, I've lived here all my life. My family are die-hard locals. They'll never leave, but I for one plan to get out as soon as humanly possible. I can't wait to move to New York or L.A. or one of those places where real people live."

I scanned the town one more time. "These people seem real enough to me."

"Don't let 'em fool you," she returned. "They're really brain-sucking zombies in disguise." I whipped around to stare at her, but she only laughed again. "Just kidding, but they might as well be. They're boring as the day is long and they don't even know it. Most of them have no desire to do anything other than while away their days in this burg."

"I guess it could be worse," I remarked. "Anyway, I'll be whiling away my days in this burg, too, until I pull myself out of my current funk."

She bumped my arm again. "You'll be fine. You'll get a job and earn some money and then I'll never see you again."

I spun around, but she was still grinning like that was the biggest joke ever. I dared to relax. Maybe I just made a friend. I could only hope. "I won't be doing any of that until I find a place to stay tonight. Otherwise, I'll be living on this bench for the rest of eternity."

"Is that all you're worried about? That's easy. You can rent a room from Charlie."

My head shot up. "Really? How do I do that?"

She pointed to a large house across the street. It sat a little back from the main flow of traffic. "He runs a boardinghouse right over there. You just walk in and tell him you want to rent a room. Problem solved."

I blinked, too flabbergasted to think straight. It couldn't be that easy. "Is it expensive?"

She shrugged. "I think he charges fifty bucks a week."

My jaw hit the floor. "You're joking."

"Too much? I think he's open to negotiation. He's a decent guy. I could introduce you if you want."

"Great!" I jumped up. "Thanks! I really appreciate it."

She waved her hand at nothing. "Cool it, champ. What's the rush? Sit down and shoot the breeze for a while—unless you're trying to get rid of me."

I dropped onto the bench in a hurry. "Not at all! Thanks. I really appreciate it."

She cracked a grin. "You said that already. If we're going to be friends, you're going to have to stop saying that."

I froze. "Friends?"

"Unless you don't want to be," she went on. "I understand."

"No!" I blurted out. "I'd like to be…it's just that…well, I've never been very good at making them—not to mention keeping them."

"Me, either." She crossed her arms and her legs. "I always see it as similar to that new photo-distorting app. Everybody gushes about how great it is and how you can't live without it, but there's just something about it that escapes me. I've never been able to figure it out, so I guess that's one more of life's blessings I'll just have to survive without."

I couldn't stop staring at her. I had to do some serious mental gymnastics to accept that someone as great as this just happened to fall out of the sky onto this bench next to me. What are the odds, you know? This woman answered all my prayers I was too depressed to voice.

She swatted me again. "So tell me about yourself. What brings you to our charming little corner of nowhere?"

I winced. "I got fired from my job. I figured I might as well make a fresh start somewhere else, somewhere no one knows me."

She nodded in an understanding way. I came up with that cover story on the bus here, and now that I'd actually met someone who I didn't want to start thinking of me as a boil on the buttocks of magic, I stuck to it. She could understand me getting fired from a job easier than understanding I was a witch —or a failure as a witch—assuming she even believed in witches, which I was guessing she didn't.

"That figures. What was the job you did in your old town?" She arched one penciled eyebrow. "What town did you come from anyway?"

"Mount Freeman," I told her, "and I was a mechanic. I worked in an auto garage."

Her eyes burst open. "Yeah? That is so cool! I'm impressed. I think Eeps is looking for a new mechanic."

I opened my mouth and shut it again before I managed to make any sound. "Eeps?"

"He runs the garage." She pointed across the street toward the boardinghouse. "It's behind Charlie's, so that could work out for you. I can introduce you if you want…or Charlie can. Eeps is his brother."

"Great!" I seemed to be saying that a lot lately. Maybe I should think about saying something else once in a while.

"Welp…" She slapped her thighs with both hands. "Do you want me to take you over to Charlie's now? Then you can get settled in and decide what to do with the rest of your life."

I almost thanked her again, but I stopped myself in time. "Okay." I stood up.

I took my suitcase handle in one hand and accompanied her across the street. Every now and then, a single car or pickup truck rolled past, but not often enough. Most of the people in sight crisscrossed Main Street without even bothering to look both ways to make sure the coast was clear.

Jada halted on the doorstep. "I'll leave you here. Charlie's real nice. You won't have any problem with him. Just tell him what you want. See you around."

I shot out a hand. "Hold it! Will I see you again?"

"Sure!" She beamed up at me. "You're gonna start wondering how to get rid of me. See ya."

She walked away. I didn't even have time to turn around before the door yanked open from the inside. I whirled back the other way and found myself face to face with the hugest dude on the planet. Gray dusted his hair and scruffy beard and his enormous shoulders blocked out the doorway itself.

He compressed his lips and furrowed his brow at me, which made his beard stick out at strange angles. "Who are you?"

I took a firm grip on myself and held out my hand. "I'm Katriona Beaty. I'm new in town and I'm told you rent rooms in your house here."

"Oh," he barked. "Well, I'm on my way to the grocery store

right now. Just take your suitcase upstairs. It's the first one on the right."

He elbowed past me and started down the steps. "Hey!" I called after him. "Just…just move in…just like that?"

He waved over his shoulder, still walking away. "We'll work out the details later. Dinner's at six. Don't be late or you miss out!"

CHAPTER THREE

After lugging my suitcase up the polished wooden staircase, I parked it in the most beautifully furnished room I'd ever laid eyes on. Crisp white bedding and curtains made the whole place sparkle. Every square inch glowed, cleaned and polished to a high shine. I never dreamed a man like Charlie could keep a house this clean.

I sat down on the giant four-poster bed. So this was going to be my room for the foreseeable future. If someone had told me I would get to rent a room like this for fifty dollars a week, I wouldn't have believed it. The sun streamed through windows overlooking Main Street. A gleaming, carved dresser and armchair completed the setting.

After waiting in breathless silence for what seemed like an eternity, I took courage and went back downstairs. I left my suitcase, but when I didn't see or hear another person, I got bolder.

I peeked into an immaculate parlor also decorated in old-fashioned style. Behind that, a massive dining table took up most of the space in a rustic farm-style kitchen with a gigantic gas stove and scrubbed wooden counters. Charlie was looking more and more like my kinda landlord.

I tiptoed through the silent house. Maybe things were starting to turn my way. It couldn't hurt to go see this Eeps character and see if I could snag a job while the winds of fortune were with me.

I left through the front door and wound up back on Main Street. Jada said Eeps's shop was behind Charlie's. I walked around the block to a back street lined with charming little houses and a few brownstones like Charlie's. Maybe this town wasn't such an ulcer after all. Now that things were looking up for me, I started to kinda like it.

I continued back up the block and heard the all-too-familiar noise of hydraulic tools and the bang of metal. A car rolled out in front of me and parked.

A large man with a buzzed military-type haircut got out and pocketed the keys in his greasy denim overalls. That must be Eeps. He looked too much like Charlie to be anyone else. Was the entire male population here this huge?

I quickened my pace to catch him before he went back inside, but about twenty feet from the shop, I heard a scream from my left. I happened to glance toward the sound and looked down a narrow alley between the buildings. In the shadows beyond, a tall, thin man crouched over a still figure lying on the ground.

The body lay flat on its face without moving. A curtain of black hair covered the features, but the strange position set my nerves on edge. I recognized at a glance that something was wrong.

The man rested his hand on the back of the person's neck, but not in a comforting, concerned way. He looked like he was checking the person's pulse, but his hard, unmoving countenance sent a quiver of alarm through my veins.

Without thinking, I rotated and stepped into the alley. "Is everything okay?"

The man looked up. His clear, gray eyes shot straight to my guts. I looked down at the figure. From this vantage, I could see it was a woman. She had wide hips and her shirt was cut in curves to show off her waist. A trail of blood ran out from under her head, staining the pavement.

I looked up at the man and his features twisted in a sickening mask of malice and murderous hatred. He started to stand up. On instinct, I spread my fingers to call up my magical power. It was the only weapon I had to stop him from doing to me what he did to this woman.

The man tensed. He flexed his knees to spring, but at that moment, a catapulting missile rocketed out of nowhere and collided with him. Another man hit the stranger with colossal force and bowled him over.

I stared in shock as the two men tumbled over and over each other. They rolled farther into the alley, away from the woman's body. They smashed into a dumpster with the killer underneath.

He shot out both arms and seized his attacker by the shirt. He pitched the newcomer off without much effort and the stranger sailed away. He hit the opposite wall and bounced. I gaped in utter horror as he landed on all fours and transformed before my very eyes.

His spine bent and his head exploded. It stretched into a snout and brown fur burst out all over his skin. Thus changing into a monstrous roaring bear, he launched for the killer. He cracked his jaws and bared his deadly fangs to tear the killer apart.

The killer pounced to his feet and landed in a crouch. The bear came within a few feet of ripping him limb from limb when the killer shot off the ground with unnatural speed. He sailed upward a lot higher than any man should be able to jump. I gaped as he levitated three floors—yes, three floors—onto the roof of the nearest building.

The bear landed where the guy just squatted, looked around, and bellowed in rage. The killer stared down at him for a moment and then vanished out of sight.

The bear swiveled and my insides turned to water when he

locked his small, piercing eyes on me. He growled low in his massive chest. Then he lowered his head between his giant shoulders. He paced across the alley and halted next to the woman's body.

The bear snuffled his nose into her hair and his growls changed. They took on a pathetic kind of whimper. He nuzzled the woman's neck, cast one last scrutinizing look at me, and then trotted off somewhere. I didn't see where.

I stood rooted to the spot until he left. All thought of going to Eeps's shop flew right out of my head. What the heck just happened? I didn't have to ask.

Bear shifters. In the space of a minute, everything that happened clicked in my mind. Bear shifters. This town was populated with bear shifters. No wonder it didn't turn up on the internet. Charlie. Eeps. They were all shifters. I even recognized a few others on Main Street. They all bore the same stamp of size, bulk, and immovable stubbornness.

The feeling of optimism, like things might be finally going right for me, dissolved and left me cold. Of all the towns on the planet, I had to blunder into the one occupied by bear shifters—the people who most hated witches of every kind.

I didn't have enough money to leave. I was living in a bear shifter's house. I was planning—maybe—to get a job working for one.

Jada was the only person I'd seen since I first got off the bus that I could be absolutely certain was NOT a bear shifter. She was too thin and too angular—and so was the killer, so he wasn't a shifter, either. No way. And anyway, if he had been one, he would have fought that other shifter as a bear. That was how bear shifters dealt with each other. They settled their disputes with teeth and claws.

I had to get out of this town. I had to somehow find a way to get on the bus to the next town. I had to...I woke from my stupor and wound up looking down at the body again. Whoever she was, she was dead as a doormat. I couldn't leave her lying here. I had to…

I stumbled the few steps to where she lay, but when I squatted down to study her, I stopped myself from touching her. This was a crime scene, and I was the only witness to that fight between the killer and the bear—at least, I assumed he was the killer. He sure looked like one.

I looked up, thinking fast. I should call 911. I put my hand into my pocket for my phone when a siren screeched down the street. A cop car skidded to a halt and blocked the alley.

A uniformed officer jumped out, pulled his sidearm, and pointed it at me. "Freeze! Don't move! Get your hands above your head! Turn around and get down on the ground."

My hands shot up of their own accord. I straightened up and started to say I didn't kill that woman, but the cop wasn't listening. He kept bellowing for me to turn around and get down on the ground.

Without thinking, I took a step toward him. I had to explain. I had to tell him what I'd seen, but he reacted in a flash. He planted his legs and thundered at the top of his lungs. "Don't come any closer or I'll shoot! Get down on the ground! Put your hands behind your head."

Before I knew what happened, his partner hopped out of the car and pulled his sidearm, too. They both held me at gunpoint yelling their heads off. Their voices echoed down the alley and confused me even more.

My heart flipped. They couldn't shoot me. They couldn't think I killed that woman. My life might be someone's idea of a bad joke, but it couldn't turn out like this. It couldn't.

I gulped. I had no choice but to kneel down and let them haul me away for a murder I didn't commit. Tears stung my eyes, and this time, I didn't have the mental fortitude to blink them away.

I started to turn when someone rushed around the two cops. I stared in blank disbelief as a large man blocked their guns with his body. It was the guy from the coffee shop, the Carhartt-wearing guy who laughed at me when my spell went wrong.

He held up one hand to me and one to the cops. "It's all right, Simon. Put your gun away, Tony. Everything's all right. I saw the whole thing. She didn't do anything. She just turned up at the wrong time." He turned to me. "You can put your arms down. I know you didn't do anything."

I gaped up at him, too stupid with surprise and relief to speak. The two cops frowned. They took a moment to lower their guns. "You didn't see her. She was touching the body."

"I was not!" I screeched. "I never touched her. I was about to call the police, you flat-footed dunce!"

The cops stiffened and frowned even deeper, but the big guy only laughed. "Chill out, Tony. I saw her. She just showed up here. Put your guns away. Don't make me tell you again."

My head shot up and I stared at him even harder. Who in the Sam Hill was this guy?

At his word, both cops holstered their weapons. The one he called Tony shrugged and looked away. "If you say so."

"I do say so. She didn't do anything." He rotated to face me. "Don't worry about it. I saw everything."

I froze. "Everything?"

"Yes, everything. You have nothing to worry about."

Simon rubbed his chin. "We still have to work up the scene, you know."

The big guy waved behind me. "Go right ahead." He took hold of my elbow and steered me out of the way.

The two cops advanced on the body. One of them started taking pictures on his phone while the other made a call. The big guy guided me to the cop car, but he stopped short of taking me out of the alley.

A few minutes later, the Crime Lab people showed up and started taping off the scene, dusting everything for fingerprints, and taking pictures of everything. After a moment, they turned the body over.

Blood and grime smeared the woman's sharp features. Even under all that muck, I recognized the unmistakable cheekbones and strong jaw of another bear shifter, a female.

Her black, unseeing eyes stared up at the sky and a gaping, bloody hole showed where all the flesh had been ripped out of her neck. A swollen flap of muscle and tissue revealed the severed vessels and windpipe underneath.

I covered my mouth to hold back a wave of nausea, but the big guy turned me away from the sight. He bent low and murmured to me under his breath. "You'll have to give a statement to the cops and they'll probably want to fingerprint you and all that stuff, but it will be okay. I know you didn't kill her."

"Thank you." I took advantage of the moment to broach the obvious question. "Who are you? How do you know these cops?"

He burst into a grin. "I'm Jamie Braeburn, and both of these two are my cousins. They trust me. If I say I saw the whole thing, they know I wouldn't lie about it."

I stiffened, but I stopped myself from pulling away from him, considering he just saved my bacon from arrest and probably worse. "You're a bear shifter just like that guy who attacked the killer. All these people are bear shifters—which means those cops are shifters, too. Aren't they? You're a shifter. Admit it."

He arched his eyebrows, peering down at me. He spoke in an undertone so only I could hear him. "And you're a witch, so let's not start off on the wrong foot by calling each other nasty names."

My jaw hit the sidewalk all over again. "How do you know about that?"

"I saw you at the coffee shop," he breathed. "Don't you remember? It would have been pretty hard to miss the volcanic eruption of chocolate milk all over the neighborhood." My head snapped up to stare at him again, but he only laughed. "Now you tell me *your* name. That's the civil thing to do."

I looked away. "Katriona Beaty."

"Do yourself a big favor, Katriona," he whispered, "and don't tell these guys or anyone else that you're a witch. Just keep it to yourself. People around here have a thing about witches."

I looked away again. He didn't have to tell me. "But not you, right? You're different. Isn't that what you were about to say?"

"I *am* different because I've had a little more exposure to the world than most people around here. Just take my word for it and keep it under your hat. It won't affect the murder investigation either way. You can tell the truth about what you saw and just happen to leave out that irrelevant detail."

I took another look at the guy. For someone who looked and acted and carried himself like a farmer, he didn't think or talk like one. He acted like he'd seen the world and probably gotten a significant higher education.

At the mention of murder, my attention switched back to the body. "He killed her, didn't he? That guy I saw bending over her killed her."

"You don't know that," he murmured in my ear. "Stick to what you saw and don't jump to conclusions."

"You say you saw everything," I countered. "How did you see the fight?"

He pointed across the street to a row of houses. "I was over there meeting someone. I saw it through the window."

I would have liked to ask more, but Simon sauntered over. "Jamie, man, we need you to sign the death certificate." He held out a square of paper and a pen.

Jamie accompanied him to the body. He stepped right over the cordon tape and examined the body with unusual attention. He pried back the dead woman's eyelids and squinted at her pupils before he scribbled something on the paper and handed it back to Simon.

Jamie straightened up. "I don't see any other signs of trauma, but I'll have to do a full autopsy just to make sure. Tell Abbott I'll be around to the morgue tomorrow or the next day."

He strolled back to me and stopped. "I have to go. Give me your phone number and I'll text you mine. Let me know if you need me to talk to the detective for you, but I know the guy and I'll be giving a statement, too, so it shouldn't be a problem."

I hauled my eyes up to his face. Everything about him conflicted with everything I knew about bear shifters. "You're... you're a doctor?"

He snorted again. "I'm THE doctor. I'm the only doctor this town has, and while we're on the subject, just about everyone in this town knows me. I was doing a home visit for one of my patients when I saw the fight. That's what I was doing over there in that house." He glanced over his shoulder toward the crime scene. "Just a word of caution. The detective is human. He's one of the few in this town, so I would think twice about telling him a bear shifter attacked that guy. He might not take it too well, if you know what I mean."

He stood there like the Washington freakin' Monument while I gaped at him in dumb shock. This was all too much for my tiny brain to comprehend.

Simon came back. "I need to take your statement now, miss."

Jamie nudged me. "Give me your number."

I repeated it automatically. When Simon said, "Now can you tell me what happened?" I looked up and Jamie was gone.

CHAPTER FOUR

I sat on the bench in front of the bus stop. Hurtler's Gulch looked a whole heck of a lot different to me now than it had just a few hours ago—not that it had changed in that time.

How could I have been so stupid not to notice shifters walking all over the place? Just think. They did their grocery shopping and filled up their cars with gas at the station on the corner. They went about their lives as if being bear shifters was the most normal thing in the world. In this town, it was.

After Simon gave me Detective Abbott's business card and told me not to leave town until the detective told me I could, I somehow managed to stagger back here, but I couldn't bring myself to cross the street to Charlie's house.

All my stuff was in the upstairs bedroom—that bedroom I'd admired so much, the bedroom I thought I was lucky to get to live in. Charlie was a shifter, too. Anyone with an eye in their head could see that.

Even as I sat here avoiding the boardinghouse like the plague, I knew I would end up going back there. I had to. I had nowhere else to go. I would stay there and I would wind up working for Eeps, but I couldn't go around the block to face him, either. For some reason, I imagined I had it tattooed on my forehead that I was such a failure as a witch that I didn't realize all these people were bear shifters.

That was just ridiculous, though, wasn't it? A smart person—a smart witch—would play it off and pretend she'd known all along. So what was I doing sitting on this bench feeling sorry for myself? I felt worse about not realizing the obvious than being accused of killing that woman.

I glanced to my left. Another rusty old pickup angled into the filling station. I'd counted a total of fifteen rusty old pickups driving through town since I'd been sitting here. That came to a grand total of seventy percent rusty old pickups out of all the vehicles I'd seen in this town. The rusty old pickup truck seemed to be the bear shifter's vehicle of choice.

I started to turn around when someone flopped onto the bench next to me. Jada crashed into my shoulder. "I've been looking all over for you. I just bumped into Carmen Albertson. She's Eeps's receptionist and she said you hadn't been over to the shop yet. What's the matter? Did you get cold feet?"

Before I could let myself hesitate, I swiveled around and blurted out, "Do you know Jamie Braeburn?"

Her eyes popped. "What about him?"

I took a deep breath. I didn't want to tell anyone what I'd seen in that alley. I wanted to forget the whole incident, but I had to confide in someone. Maybe Jada would think I was out of my natural mind. I wouldn't blame her.

Throwing caution to the wind, I poured out the whole story from start to finish. I didn't leave out a single detail—not the guy shifting into a bear, not Jamie stepping in and saving my hide from arrest or worse, not the woman with her throat torn out.

When I finished, Jada faced front and gazed across the street. "So you found out about 'em. That didn't take you near as long as I thought it would."

"You know about them?" I exclaimed. "You know about all these people being shifters?"

"Of course," she returned. "Everybody knows. The Braeburns are huge in this town. They're everywhere. You can't walk down the dang street without tripping over fifteen of 'em. They own all the land around here." She sliced her finger over the wooded hills beyond the town. "Jamie went away to medical school, but he came back in the end. We're lucky to have a doctor as knowledgeable and dedicated as he is, but most of the bear shifters never leave town. They're lucky if they graduate from high school. The good news is that he knows more about shifters than anyone so he can doctor them. They don't have to rely on a human doctor who might freak over their physiology. They all trust him, and for good reason."

I gaped at the side of her face. "You make it sound so…so normal."

"It is. It's normal for this town. Heck, there are more Braeburns around here than anything else. You'd have your work cut out for you finding a real, bona fide human in this town… besides you, that is."

She cracked a grin at me and I blushed. "He said Detective Abbott is human and that I shouldn't tell him the truth about the shifter attacking that guy. Is that true? How could Detective Abbott work here and not know the truth about the Braeburns?"

Jada shrugged. "I don't concern myself with what Detective Abbott knows and what he doesn't know. I guarantee you he knows about the Braeburns and what they are, though." She grinned even wider. "He would have to because they're always getting in fights and occasionally killing each other. There is nothing going on in this town that he doesn't know about. I can promise you that."

I frowned. "I wonder why Jamie said that, then."

"Maybe because that bear shifter you saw was one of his relatives and he doesn't want the guy to get in trouble."

I whipped around fast. "Are you serious?"

"I would bet cold hard cash they're related. There isn't a bear shifter on this whole mountain that isn't related to the Braeburns one way or the other. I bet he was trying to protect the guy."

I slumped and slapped my hand to my forehead. "How in the name of God did I get myself into this?"

"Just do your best when it comes to Detective Abbott. If Jamie saw the fight, he'll back your story. Detective Abbott trusts him. Jamie Braeburn doesn't lie. Everybody knows that. You have nothing to worry about."

I hazarded a sidelong peek at her face. "What about you? Is your family okay with living in the same town with so many bear shifters?"

"Well, we don't have much of a choice, do we?" she returned. "Maybe we've been living here so long we're just used to it."

I shook my head. My brain still lagged at catching up with the rest of the world. I scrutinized Hurtler's Gulch, trying to grasp all the tangled threads that made up this town.

Jada woke me from my thoughts by bumping my arm. "You better get back to Charlie's or you'll miss dinner."

I jerked around to find her smiling at me. "How do you know about that?"

She rolled her eyes to heaven. "Girl, please. If there is one thing you need to learn about this town, it's that there are no secrets—anywhere. Now come on. When Charlie says latecomers miss out, he isn't kidding."

She picked me up and set me on my feet. Before I knew what was happening, we were walking across the street. The boardinghouse got nearer and nearer. In a minute, I would be on the steps with nowhere to go but inside—into that den of bears.

Jada halted on the sidewalk. "I gotta go home, too. I'll see you tomorrow. I'll go over to Eeps's shop around ten, so make sure you're working there by then or there's mud on your face."

She squeezed my arm and abandoned me to my fate. I inhaled a shaky breath and pushed the door open. Whatever I was expecting, the succulent smell of roast beef and cheesy pasta definitely wasn't it. A spurt of saliva hit my tongue and my stomach spasmed. I hadn't had anything but hot chocolate since last night.

Irresistible gravity towed me down the hall to the kitchen. I walked in and almost collided with Jamie Braeburn. His towering bulk blocked the entrance. He looked down at me with those piercing eyes of his.

I stopped on a dime. "What are you doing here?"

"Nice to see you again, too. Come on in. We're just about to eat."

He slotted onto a bench at the table. Two other people sat across from him, both women. The first was nearly as tall as Charlie and she looked to be about thirty-five, but her hair was just as black and sleek as a woman half her age. The other one looked about my age, but she was a whole lot bigger than me.

Before I could move, Charlie entered through the back door. He spotted me and bent over the oven. "You're here. Good. I can't stand lateness, especially at meals. Sit down. What do you want to drink?"

I glanced at the table. There was nowhere to sit but next to Jamie. "Uh…" I stammered. "Water, I guess."

"Another health nut," the older woman interjected and everyone laughed.

Charlie barged in front of me and put a thick cutting board on the table. Piles of carved, juicy beef sprawled for all the world to see and my stomach gave another shudder. Man, I was hungry.

I sat down on the bench as far down as I dared to keep plenty of room between me and Jamie, but he bumped into me reaching for the meat. Charlie put a casserole pan of cheesy pasta next to the cutting board and pushed me closer to Jamie. "Make room, bony. Where am I supposed to sit?"

I slid along the bench, but there was barely enough room for me between these two giant men. They sandwiched me between them and their elbows kept banging into me while they helped themselves to the food.

The women didn't hold back, either. Everybody dug in big time. In the space of a few seconds, I started to understand what everyone had been telling me. If I didn't start fending for myself, there would be nothing left to eat.

I had to knock Charlie's chiseled arms aside to reach the meat, but he didn't seem to notice. He took it as understood that the meal would turn into a wrestling match.

I stabbed a massive slab of beef and scooped a mountain of pasta onto my plate just to ensure I wouldn't have to go to battle again anytime soon. I took hold of my fork when the older woman picked up a pitcher of water from the far end of the table. Lemon slices and mint leaves floated among the ice chips.

She poured water into my glass and set it in front of me. "Jamie, you clod! You didn't give her anything to drink."

"I forgot." He stuffed a piece of crispy beef into his mouth and chewed while he talked.

"Do you eat here often?" I hoped the question didn't sound too rude, but I wanted to know right out front if I would be encountering him at the dinner table on a regular basis.

"Only when Charlie invites me. He's my uncle on my father's side, in case you're wondering. Jenny is my aunt on my mother's side…" He indicated the older woman. "And Patricia is my cousin from her older brother."

"We live here," Jenny told me, "so we eat here all the time."

The others all laughed again, but I didn't see what was so funny. I started to bow over my plate to hide my discomfort when Jamie spoke up again. "Katriona's uncomfortable because she just discovered Hurtler's Gulch is a shifter town," he told the others. "She spotted Eli shifting when he attacked Rickards earlier."

The others nodded like they knew all about it. I checked one face after the other. When I swiveled around to look at Jamie, he was gazing back at me with sparkling eyes. "Did you tell them?" I asked.

"I didn't have to. The news was all over town within minutes. Stuff like that never stays quiet for long."

I lowered my gaze to my plate. "So I keep hearing."

"Rickards is a scumbag," Patricia muttered. "Someone should have taken him out long ago. I'm glad Eli took a stab at him even if he didn't succeed."

I stared at her. "You know that guy—the killer?"

"No one knows for certain if it was Rickards that killed Sophie," Jamie interrupted. "I told you it's never a good idea to jump to conclusions. We can all hate Rickards until we're blue in the face. That doesn't mean he killed her."

"Well, Eli didn't," Jenny fired back. "I will never believe that. He loved her."

I stared at one person after another. "You…you knew her—the victim? Who was she?"

The others looked away—all of them. Not one of them would meet my gaze. My eyes snapped from one person to the other. She was one of them. She had to be. They just didn't want to say so to a stranger.

I read the situation in the blink of an eye. It was bad enough I found out about them. Now I was up to my eyelids in all their personal family business. That must be a nightmare for a close-knit clan like them.

All at once, Charlie launched to his feet. "None of this will bring Sophie back. Now Eli's gone AWOL and no one will ever bring Rickards back. We might as well all go on with our lives."

"Without Sophie, you mean," Jenny remarked.

Charlie shrugged, pulling open the fridge. "You dance with the devil, you pay the price. Anybody could see that coming a mile away."

"What do you mean?" I asked.

Charlie pretended not to hear and neither of the women answered.

"Have you heard from Detective Abbott yet?" Jamie asked me.

I spun around to stare at him. "No. Why? Should I have?"

He shrugged. "I thought you would have. It isn't like him to leave a witness alone this long."

"A suspect, you mean," I corrected.

"Get on with you," Jenny exclaimed. "You're not a suspect."

"Really?" I countered. "Tell Simon and Tony that."

Jenny's eyes sliced to Jamie and he shrugged again. "They got the wrong idea when they found her at the scene."

"I hope you told 'em it wasn't true," Charlie cut in.

"I tried, but you know what they're like."

"Overenthusiastic," Jenny answered.

"Fanatical," Patricia added and everyone laughed again.

Jenny pushed back her plate and stood up. "We have to get going. Thanks for dinner, Charlie."

She and Patricia both carried their plates to the sink. Jamie pushed his plate away. "I better go, too." He bumped my shoulder. "You come and see me at the morgue tomorrow after you talk to Detective Abbott."

I turned around to ask what he meant about the morgue, but he'd already walked out. His heavy boots clumped down the hall and the front door slammed.

That left me alone with Charlie, who was busy doing something or other in the pantry behind the kitchen. I guessed that was the end of dinner.

I picked up my plate and started to gather the dirty dishes off the table. Hills of food remained on the board and in the casserole pan, but not one of the diners had left so much as a crumb on their plates.

I stacked them and was in the process of collecting the cutlery when Charlie returned. The moment he saw what I was doing, he charged me. "Oh, no, you don't! Out! Get out of my kitchen!" He seized the dishes from me and herded me into the hall. "Good night!"

"Hey!" I yelled after his disappearing form. "I was just trying to help. Also, I haven't paid you the rent yet."

His disembodied voice drifted to my ear from far away. "Leave it on the hall table. See you in the morning. Breakfast is at seven-thirty. Don't be late!"

Another door slammed. I blinked around me at the silent corridor. He didn't tell me how much rent money to leave—did he want a week's worth or an entire month?

With another blank look around, I climbed the stairs to that room—my room. It welcomed the exhausted soul to wash all its cares away in blessed, blessed sleep and that's exactly what I did.

CHAPTER FIVE

I took a long time falling asleep that first night, but in the end, my new bedroom's peaceful, protective atmosphere lulled me into one of the best night's sleep I could remember in a long time. It pervaded Charlie's whole house. The place oozed comfort and protection, like nothing could come near me there.

I woke up refreshed in the morning. I lounged in bed soaking up the glorious vibes. I actually started to believe I was on vacation in some tropical spa when I remembered breakfast.

I lunged for my phone and checked the time. Seven o'clock. I better hustle or I would miss the food entirely. I hopped out of bed, grabbed a shower and changed my clothes, and made it to the kitchen just as Jenny and Patricia were sitting down.

Jenny beamed at me. "Punctual. You'll go far in this town."

I made a face. "Gotta start paying the rent first."

Charlie called over from the stove where he worked over several sizzling skillets on the giant range. He wore a spotless white apron over his jeans, a black t-shirt hugging his ripped chest and shoulders. "You already paid it. I found that money you left on the hall table. You didn't need to leave so much. I can use the excess for power and internet."

"I paid for this week," I told him while I sat down at the table with the two women. "It's next week and the week after that I'm worried about. I gotta hit the bricks this morning and find me a job."

"Do you have any prospects?" Patricia asked. "What are your skills?"

"I'm an auto mechanic. I hear Eeps might be hiring. That's my first port of call."

The two women stared at me with huge eyes. "Quit fooling. You are not!"

I nodded. "Got my certificate from the Mount Freeman Community College and four years' experience at Jimmy's on Fourth Street. I even have references to prove it."

"Eeps will snap you up, then." Charlie dumped a mountain of scrambled eggs, a log cabin of bacon strips, and another heap of fried sausages in front of me. "You better eat up. He'll probably want to put you to work as soon as you show your face in the door."

I stared up at him. "Really? Is he under the water?"

"He was already short-handed and working seventy hours a week," Patricia told me. "He'll be even more behind now that Eli has gone on the run."

My head shot up. Eli. That was the shifter guy I saw at the crime scene. "Why did he go on the run if he didn't kill that girl —Sophie?"

"He couldn't have killed her," Jenny countered. "He's her brother."

"That never stopped anybody before," Charlie rumbled. "Him running off like that doesn't look very good, does it?"

I turned to look up at him. "Was Sophie—I hope this doesn't sound rude coming from me—was she a Braeburn? Was she one of your clan?"

Charlie nudged me down the bench again and wedged himself in next to me. Then he attacked his food with all four limbs. "Why would it sound rude? She was my niece."

I shook my head and stabbed my fork into a sausage. "I don't think I'll ever get all these relationships straight."

"Don't worry about it," Jenny told me. "Just tell Eeps when you go there that you have to run to the station to give your statement to Detective Abbott. Just get it out of the way."

My head swiveled around the other way to look at her. I kept turning one way and then the other to address one person after another. "How does everyone know every detail of my personal business?"

She only shrugged. "Jamie said last night that you had to give the detective a statement."

I pushed the food around my plate, but I couldn't make much headway with it. Too many crazy puzzle pieces kept rearranging themselves in my head. "I better get over to the shop. Jada Hooper said she would meet me there at ten o'clock and make sure I was on the job."

The others froze, staring at me. Their cheery expressions dissolved, and a chill fell over the room. Charlie's features solidified into a wall of immovable granite. The two women glared at me and then exchanged glances with each other.

My gaze darted around the table. "What's the matter? Did I say something wrong?"

Charlie hmphed under his breath and jabbed his fork into a sausage with murderous fury. "Of course not."

Jenny compressed her lips. The face that once looked so kind and welcoming and sympathetic changed into a mask of venomous hatred. "We just don't like the Hoopers very much. You might say we have an old grudge against them."

"What grudge is that?"

"We just don't like them," Patricia added. "That's how it's always been. The Braeburns and the Hoopers don't mix. That's just the way it is."

"That bastard Rickards is Jada's brother," Jenny snarled. "I bet he did kill Sophie. I don't care what Jamie says. Someone will prove that Rickards killed her and then the Braeburns will have even more reason to drive those vermin out of town."

I blinked at her in astonishment. "That's harsh."

"Yeah, well, I'd stay away from Jada if I was you," Patricia remarked. "She's the worst of them all."

"She seemed real nice to me," I ventured. "She was the one who told me about this house and about Eeps probably wanting to hire a new mechanic."

Jenny curled her lip in a grimace. "She can be real nice when it suits her. She's a snake in the grass. You mark my words."

"If she's so bad," I persisted, "how come she never says anything bad about the Braeburns? Since I met her yesterday, she's said nothing but nice things about your whole clan."

Jenny looked away. "She's a liar. She's a witch."

That word sent a jolt of alarm up my spine. A witch. No one in this town knew I was a witch—except Jamie. I better watch my step and make sure none of them ever found out.

Then again, Jada said this town had no secrets. Jamie said stuff like that never stayed quiet for long. How long before these people turned on me, too? The Braeburns might be the nicest people in the world, but shifters harbored a notorious hatred of witches. Everybody knew that.

I pushed back my plate. "I better go get myself a job. Thank you for the breakfast, Charlie."

"You didn't eat anything!" he yelled after me.

I bolted out of the house and made tracks for Eeps's shop. I pulled up in front of the garage just as the huge proprietor was hanging a *Mechanic Wanted* sign on the front window.

I barged right up to him before I had a chance to lose my nerve. "I'm a mechanic."

He scowled down his nose at me. "You don't look like much of a mechanic to me."

I pulled my resumé and Jimmy's reference letter out of my handbag. "I'm fully qualified and I have four years' experience. I can start immediately and I have a very strong work ethic."

He narrowed his eyes at the two documents. "Is that a fact?"

"I have to tell you, though, that I witnessed a fight yesterday between Eli Braeburn and Rickards Hooper." I waved my hand at nothing. "I'm sure you heard all about it. Anyway, I have to go give a statement to Detective Abbott…sometime. I just thought I'd let you know up front in case that affects your decision on whether to hire me."

He trained his flashing brown eyes on me. These Braeburns had an uncanny knack for piercing someone to the marrow with their sharp eyes. "I did hear about it."

I shuffled my feet and cast a longing glance toward the garage. "So…can I have the job?"

He folded up my resumé and letter and tucked them into his jumpsuit pocket. "I tell you what. You go along to the police station right now and give Detective Abbott your statement. Take all the time you need getting your business straightened out. I'll give you today off and you can start bright and early tomorrow morning as soon as you finish stuffing yourself on Charlie's sausage."

My head shot up to stare at him, but this time, his eyes twinkled and he cracked a grin. I should have known Eeps would have heard all about me staying at Charlie's. News like that traveled through the freakin' airwaves in this town. For all I knew, these Braeburns had a dang psychic connection and didn't have to talk to each other at all.

My shoulders sagged and I puffed out my cheeks in a shaky sigh. "Thanks. I really appreciate it."

"Not as much as I'm gonna appreciate a fully qualified mechanic with a strong work ethic." He took the sign off the window. "I'll see you tomorrow morning."

CHAPTER SIX

I hurried away from Eeps's shop with my heart in my mouth. I never imagined getting a job would be so easy. Landing at Charlie's and now this—I might be tempted to start thinking that—shifter town or not—things were looking pretty rosy for me right about now.

The simple fact that I was on my way to the police station to give a statement chilled my enthusiasm, though. I was a suspect in a murder investigation. I couldn't get complacent with that hanging over my head.

I didn't even know where the stupid police station was. I would have to ask someone. I turned the corner onto Main Street and nearly had a heart attack when I slammed into Jada coming the other way. I bounced back in surprise. "Holy-moly, you scared the pants off me!"

She stood back and dragged her eyes down my body. "I hate to tell you this, but your pants are still on."

"You know what I mean," I countered. "You scared me."

"You were a million miles away." She cocked an eyebrow at me. "You're going the wrong way. You're supposed to be on your way to Eeps's to apply for a job."

"I just came from there." I stepped past her. "I got the job and now I have to go to the police station to give a statement to Detective Abbott, but since I don't even know where the place is, I could be wandering around this loopy town for the rest of the week looking for it."

Jada took a step to my side and followed me. "Don't be so dramatic. Come on, I can take you there."

I shot her a sidelong glance, but I didn't feel right about telling her to leave me alone. She had been the nicest to me of everyone since I first turned up in this town. "So—I discovered the Braeburns don't like you very much. They've got nothing nice to say about you."

Her head snapped around and she gasped. Then she exploded with laughter. "Is that so? I would so LOVE to hear what they've been telling you about me."

I faced front to hide my burning cheeks. "They say you're a liar and a witch and a snake in the grass. They think your brother Rickards killed Sophie Braeburn and that Eli Braeburn was right to attack Rickards when I spotted him kneeling next to her dead body." I rounded on her, hissing through gritted teeth. "Why didn't you tell me? How could you sit there and listen to me spilling my guts about everything that happened and not tell me that you were related to that…that guy?"

She regarded me through calm, understanding eyes. "Maybe because I didn't want you to tar me with the same brush the Braeburns do. Maybe I like you and I thought we could be friends without letting all those prejudices get in the way. It's hard enough to make friends in this town when everyone my age belongs to the Braeburn clan."

I started walking again. I didn't know what to think, but I wanted more than anything to believe her. I didn't want to lose the one friend and ally I had in this town. "They think you'll say anything to twist a person around your little finger."

I would have kept walking, but she grabbed my arm and pulled me to a stop. "Listen, sweetheart, if you don't want me as a friend, just tell me. I'll go back to my lonely life sobbing into my cappuccino and you can go get up to your eyelashes in grease at Eeps's. I don't care. Honestly, I don't. I have better things to do than trying to cozy up to someone who thinks I'm the devil incarnate."

I pulled my head in quick. "I didn't mean that. I do want to be friends with you. You've been nothing but nice to me. It's just that I'm the prime suspect in the murder investigation of a woman I didn't even know. I just fell up to my armpits in this blinkin' feud between a whole army of bear shifters and…" I waved at her, but words failed me.

She suddenly exploded in laughter again. "Don't sweat it, girl. Come on. Go give the detective your statement and then we can go get some pancakes."

I studied the sidewalk passing under my feet. "I'm not hungry. I'm too full of sausage."

She laughed even harder. "You better watch yourself staying at Charlie's or we'll be rolling your chubby backside down the street."

I rolled my eyes. "I'll definitely have to start working out or pretty soon, I'll start to look like Charlie. I'll be going out for the Arnold Schwarzenegger prize for Frankenstein Female of the Year."

Jada laughed so hard she slapped her thighs and hugged her ribs. "Stop it! I can't stand it."

I had to smile at her. I liked making her laugh. In all the years I spent in the Mount Freeman coven, I never had a real friend. I didn't realize that until right now. The other witches in the coven never acted friendly—not to me, anyway. They were too formal and too serious about being serious witches and had no room in their lives for someone who apparently wasn't serious witch material.

I never had anyone in my life to just mess around with and have a casual, friendly, fun time with. I liked it—a lot. I wanted it to keep on going. I would much rather go get pancakes with Jada than go into the police station.

She stopped in front of a building. I couldn't exactly miss the giant sign out front declaring to the world that this was *Hurtler's Gulch Police Department*.

I also couldn't miss all the uniformed bear shifters going in and out through the front entrance and driving to and from the parking lot in squad cars. If I went in there, I would be walking straight into bear shifter central. Anybody could see that.

Jada touched my elbow. "I'll catch you later, okay? How about we meet up outside the grocery store about lunchtime? You probably have some stuff to get for your room at Charlie's, and if you don't, we can just fool around for the rest of your day off. You probably won't be getting another one anytime soon. Eeps will be cracking the whip on you come the morning."

I cast a long gaze down Main Street. "Probably."

"So…" she hedged. "Do you want to meet up later?"

"Sure. I'll see you there."

She gave me one last brilliant grin. The minute she walked away, a thousand misgivings crowded into my brain. Was that exchange just an act Jada used to get in my good books? What possible reason could she have to do that? What could she possibly stand to gain by making friends with me?

I shuddered remembering all the twisted threads weaving through this town. How in the name of Pete did I ever get so lucky, yet so unlucky? No one but me could wind up submerged up to her neck in this morass of confused loyalties, hatreds, murder, and competing narratives.

I shook myself out of my funk. All I had to do was go inside the police station and give Detective Abbott my statement. Everyone kept telling me that Jamie would back up my version of events. Then I would be cleared. I could go shopping and ride off into the sunset of working a steady job, living in a beautiful house, eating awesome food, and living my little old life.

I kept my head down so I wouldn't see all the shifters around me. I tried to make myself inconspicuous as I walked up to the reception desk. Unfortunately for me, I had to look up to address the receptionist. That was when I noticed that she was a shifter, too.

She smiled at me. Her broad, round face reminded me of a big, shining moon with strong cheekbones, bright eyes, and a hint of knowing buried deep in her inviting expression. "Good morning. How can I help you today?"

I swallowed hard. "My name is Katriona Beaty. I need to see Detective Abbott. He…I think he might be expecting me."

She smiled even wider—if that was even possible. "By all means. I'll just page him for you."

I fidgeted, waiting for something to happen next, but when I looked around, I only spotted more shifters everywhere. They wore badges and sidearms and their muscular frames filled out their clothes with unmistakable strength and power—the men *and* the women.

While I scanned the lobby, a particularly burly character walked out of a side door. His tailored jacket formed an upside-down triangle of muscle from his huge shoulders down to his narrow waist. A holstered pistol glinted on his belt under his jacket.

He walked up to me and stuck out his hand. "Ms. Beaty? I'm Detective Mark Abbott. Thank you for coming in."

I did a double-take staring at him. He wasn't a shifter, but he was as big and powerful and as energetic as one—I guessed because he would have to be working with them all the time, not to mention arresting them when they got in fights or happened to kill one of their own relatives.

I shook his hand with my numb arm. "It's…"

He grinned down at me. He dwarfed me by a mile. He was by far the biggest man I'd seen yet in this town. He was bigger even than Charlie. "You don't have to say it's a pleasure to meet me. I know it isn't. It's never a pleasure for anyone to meet me."

My cheeks burned and I looked away. He was a whole lot nicer than I expected. I seemed to have built up this phantom idea of him as a hardened, hard-boiled bone-crusher who would go to any lengths to lock me up for Sophie's murder.

He waved toward the door through which he'd just emerged. "Shall we get this over with? Then you can go on with your day."

I glanced behind me toward the security checkpoint. Everyone going into or out of the police station had to empty their pockets and step through the scanner to get inside. "Don't I have to go through the checkpoint?"

"Not if I say you don't. Follow me. We can talk in my office."

He held the door open for me. The door led into a blank corridor that ended in a blank stairwell. At the bottom, we entered a bay of cubicles. On the other side of that, he opened a glass door to a glass-walled office like any other.

He waved me toward a chair and sat down at his desk. He moved some papers around while he talked. "I've already taken Jamie Braeburn's statement and he leaves me in little doubt about what happened."

I stiffened in my chair. "Then what am I doing here?"

"Unfortunately, I have to take statements from all the witnesses whether I think they're involved or not. I will tell you one thing. You couldn't ask for a more reliable witness than Jamie to corroborate your story. He's very highly thought of in this town and in this department."

I bowed my head and mumbled into my collar. "So I keep hearing."

He did something on his phone and placed it face-up on the desk in front of me. "Now why don't you tell me in your own words what you saw yesterday?"

I eyed the phone and then scrutinized him. "Some people think *I* killed Sophie Braeburn. If I'm a suspect, I want to know about it upfront."

"Considering that not one single fingerprint of yours was found at the crime scene," he returned, "I think we can all assume that you aren't one."

"Your deputies—or whatever they were—held me at gunpoint at the crime scene."

He rested his arms on the desk to examine me right back. "Maybe that's because you're a stranger in town. That on its own makes you suspect for everything. The Braeburns are a very closed family. They inherently mistrust everything they don't understand. You can understand why they would immediately suspect someone they didn't know bending over the murdered body of their own cousin."

I looked away again. "Maybe they aren't the only ones."

"What do you mean?"

I shook my hair out of my eyes. "Nothing. I'm ready to give my statement now."

He tapped the phone and waved toward it. I squared my shoulders. This was it.

"I got off the bus in Hurtler's Gulch yesterday morning. I got a cup of hot chocolate at the coffee shop and then I was sitting on the bench in front of the bus stop thinking about what to do next. Jada Hooper came along and told me I could rent a room at Charlie Braeburn's boardinghouse. She also told me that Eeps Braeburn might be hiring a mechanic and I might be able to get a job there."

Detective Abbott stiffened. "You're a mechanic?"

"Yeah," I snapped. "So?"

He waved at the phone again and went back to inspecting his paperwork, but I would have to be blind to mistake the change in his expression.

"After I dropped my suitcase at Charlie's, I went around the block to go see Eeps," I went on. "I was passing the alley down the block and I heard someone scream. I looked down the alley and saw Rickards Hooper squatting next to Sophie's body. I didn't know at the time what their names were. I only found out after the fact."

I paused. I was getting closer to the part where I would have to tell him about Eli changing into a bear. Should I? Everything that happened confirmed Jada's assertion that Detective Abbott knew all about the Braeburns being shifters. If that was true, I wouldn't be telling him anything he didn't already know.

Jamie, on the other hand, seemed to think I shouldn't tell him. What if, after all his work in this police department, Detective Abbott somehow missed that tiny, insignificant detail? What if he thought I was crazy for claiming that a guy turned into a bear?

I watched Detective Abbott's reaction as I talked. The deeper I got into my tale, the more I became convinced that, for some reason, me being a mechanic made him suspect me when he didn't before he found out that I was one.

If I claimed Eli turned into a bear, that might make him suspect me even more. He might want to lock me up as a nutcase right now. The charming future I just envisioned flashed before my eyes.

Detective Abbott's head shot up and he fixed his eyes on me. "What happened then?"

"When I saw Sophie lying on her face like that, I got a feeling something was wrong. I stepped into the alley and asked if Rickards needed help. He looked up at me and then..." I stopped again.

He waited for me to say something. "And then?"

"And then...Eli Braeburn rushed past me and attacked Rickards. They fell over and crashed into the dumpster. Rickards kicked Eli off and threw him across the alley. Eli hit the other wall and landed on the ground."

Another torturous pause. "And then?"

"And then...and then Eli came charging back to attack Rickards and Rickards jumped out of the way. He jumped really high and landed on the roof. He looked down at Eli for a minute and then he vanished."

"And what did Eli do?"

Nothing in his expression or his tone told me whether my statement conflicted with Jamie's at all. Did Jamie tell Detective

Abbott about Eli shifting? Detective Abbott didn't show any surprise, either, that Rickards jumped three floors to the roof.

"Then Eli went over and checked on Sophie and then he left, too. I was all alone with Sophie's body. I went over and squatted down by the body, but I didn't touch it. I never touched anything. I was just about to take out my phone when Simon and Tony showed up and pulled their guns and started yelling their heads off telling me to get down on the ground or they would shoot me."

Detective Abbott burst into a boyish grin. "I can just imagine them doing that."

I glared at him. "You wouldn't think it was funny if it happened to you."

"You're right. I wouldn't." He pushed some more papers around. "Well, thank you for your statement. I appreciate you coming in this morning."

"So that's it? I'm done? I'm not a suspect?"

He looked up and his expression said it all. "I can't reveal any details of the investigation. I must ask you not to leave town without contacting me first."

I sat frozen to my chair. "Why not? I *am* a suspect, aren't I? What was it? Why do you suspect me? I didn't do anything."

He looked up and his big shoulders slouched. He leaned his elbows on the desk again. "I shouldn't be telling you any of this, but Sophie Braeburn's car was tampered with the night before she was killed. Someone with advanced auto mechanical skills hacked the computer system so it would break down at a certain bend in the road leading from her home to town. They ambushed her when she got out to check under the hood. They would have killed her then but her two brothers happened to be hunting in the woods at the same time. They heard her screaming and saved her life. The attacker ran off and they never found out who it was because the person was wearing a mask."

My blood turned to ice in my veins. "You think I did it? I wasn't even in this town before yesterday."

"We have only your word on that," he countered. "Can you think of anyone who can confirm your whereabouts before yesterday morning?"

My heart plummeted into my shoes. I'd been alone since I left the coven house. No one could clear my name.

"There is no way on God's green Earth that Rickards had the knowledge to tamper with Sophie's car when he can't even change a tire," Detective Abbott went on. "The only other people in town who could have tampered with Sophie's car are Eli—her brother who loved her and by all accounts would never hurt her—and Eeps himself, and we all know he didn't do it because he was Sophie's uncle and he adored her like a daughter. Besides, Eeps has two witnesses who can confirm that he was home during the night attack and several others who say he was at work in his shop when Sophie was killed."

"I have witnesses who can show I was with them when Sophie was killed, too," I squeaked. "I was talking to Jada Hooper right up until I saw Rickards in the alley."

He looked up and all hope drained from my heart. "You said yourself that you went to Charlie's first. You were alone there before you went around the block so—according to your story —you were alone when Sophie was killed."

I lowered my eyes to my hands in my lap. "I didn't kill her. I have no motive."

"Not one we know about." He pushed back his chair and stood up. "If I need to question you again, I'll let you know. Thank you again for coming in."

I kept my eyes on the floor getting the heck out of that office. I didn't want to be within a hundred miles of that guy.

I charged up the stairs and into the lobby, but just before I ran out of the station, I halted. Through the glass front doors, I got a clear view of the grocery store across the street.

It would be so easy to walk out there, meet up with Jada, and drown my sorrows in a big stack of pancakes drenched in whipped cream. That would really pack on the pounds if anything would.

Something drew me back, though. I looked over my shoulder toward the security checkpoint. A dozen shifters surrounded the scanner talking and laughing about something. Were they laughing about the fact that Detective Abbott had already identified Sophie's killer—or at least who he thought was Sophie's killer?

None of them even looked at me. They were too all-fired pleased with themselves even to see me standing there suspended between here and there.

I couldn't walk away from this. I couldn't let the sun go down on a murder accusation. I might be a boil on the backside of the magical world, but I was no killer. If the police or anyone else thought I killed Sophie, I had to do something. I just didn't know what yet.

I turned around and walked back across the lobby. I stopped halfway and surveyed my surroundings, thinking hard.

Then I had it. I strode over to the reception desk and the happy receptionist smiled at me. "Hi again."

"Hi," I said. "Can you please tell me how to get to the morgue?"

CHAPTER SEVEN

I stuck my head around the corner and nearly blinded myself looking into a room so white it seemed to be completely blank. Glaring fluorescent bulbs shone down from the ceiling. I squinted the splitting headache out of my eyes to focus on a single steel bed in the center.

Sophie's body lay on the slab and Jamie bent over her. He didn't look so much like a farmer wearing a long white lab coat, a full-body plastic apron, rubber gloves, and a full protective face shield.

He talked to himself while he poked and prodded at the body. "Victim is a twenty-one-year-old Native American female belonging to the Kiniok Tribe local to Hurtler's Gulch. She has black hair, brown eyes, and is five feet seven inches tall. She weighs one hundred and forty-five pounds. She has a distinctive hummingbird tattoo on her upper left shoulder blade and a rattlesnake tattoo around her right ankle. She has a one-inch scar on her left knee and an appendectomy scar on her lower right abdomen." He scanned the body from head to toe. "She has had Botox injections into her forehead sometime in the last two weeks and she has three abscessed injection puncture wounds on the inner surface of her left elbow."

This last detail startled me out of myself. I leaped into the room. "She does?"

He whipped around fast, jerking upright. "Holy Christmas, don't you knock?"

"The door was open and you told me to come and see you."

He blew out his breath and walked across the morgue. "You startled me."

He did something on his phone and pushed away the microphone hanging from the ceiling. I stood back. Now that I was in the same room with Sophie's body, my impulse left me. Part of me wanted to run away, but now that I was here, I found myself studying her closer in morbid fascination—literally.

"How do you know she was Native American?"

Jamie pushed a rolling table of tools out of the way. It made a crashing sound that echoed through the chilly morgue. He looked at me and scoffed. "Haven't you learned anything since you arrived in this town? If *she* was part of the Kiniok Tribe, I would have to be, too, wouldn't I? All the Braeburns are."

I looked up at him. The angular facial bones, the dark complexion, the curious knowing expression—now that he mentioned it, it seemed so obvious. I seemed to be stumbling over the obvious at every turn. "Oh, yeah."

He picked up one of his tools and leaned over Sophie's face. He opened her mouth and started poking around. "I'm guessing you being here means you gave your statement to the detective."

I rubbed my arms to warm them. "In case you're wondering, it was an unmitigated disaster."

He looked up and frowned. "How could it possibly be? I told him everything that happened."

I stiffened, staring him down. "Did you tell him about Eli shifting into a bear?"

His eyebrows jumped together in the middle. "No. Why the dickens would I want to do that?"

"Oh, I don't know. Maybe because it's the truth. Everybody

else in town seems to think Detective Abbott knows all about the Braeburns being bear shifters. What I can't figure out is why you told me to lie to him about Eli."

He frowned even deeper. "Is that it?"

"Well? Does he know about the Braeburns or not?"

"How should I know?" He went back to probing in Sophie's mouth. "It doesn't matter much."

"Except that you lied in your statement and now I've just done the same thing on your recommendation. I left out a crucial detail of that fight, a detail that could clear my name from murdering…this woman." I lowered my eyes to the body. "I shouldn't be here. I shouldn't be in the same room when you're doing the autopsy. Someone might accuse me of interfering with the investigation."

"What are you talking about?" he demanded. "You're not a suspect. I made sure of that."

I made a face. "Call yourself ill-informed, my kind friend. I am not only a suspect. I am the *prime* suspect, and I have been officially warned for the second time not to leave town. It turns out that Sophie's car was tampered with by someone with what Detective Abbott calls advanced auto mechanical skills. Someone reprogrammed the computer on her car to make it break down on a certain curve between her home and Hurtler's Gulch. The killer—or whoever—attacked her then and would have killed her if her brothers hadn't intervened." I scowled at him. "You should know all about it. The jungle grapevine should have told you the whole story."

He stood up and leveled me with a very different expression. "I knew someone attacked her and that her brothers chased the person away. I didn't know the police determined that her car had been tampered with, and I certainly didn't know the detective found out that you were a mechanic."

"But you did, right?" I sneered. "You heard in the last hour or two that I got a job at Eeps."

"Of course. He's over the moon about you."

I snorted. "Wonderful."

He put his head on one side. "Weird." Then he shrugged and went back to work.

"You want to know what's really weird?" I countered. "What's weird is that the Braeburn clan, who are supposed to be so close-knit and caring of their own, didn't even try to find out who attacked Sophie in the woods at night. That's what I find weird."

"We figured it was the Hoopers. They're always pulling underhanded stuff like that."

"So why would they target Sophie when they could have gone after you or any other Braeburn?"

"They wouldn't dare to go after me," he replied. "They know which side of the bread their butter is on. If they harmed a hair on my head, there wouldn't be a doctor within four hundred miles to cover the town. Everybody knows that."

"You know what I'm talking about," I fired back. "Someone went to a lot of trouble to make her car stop right in that one place so they would be sure to get her isolated away from her family. Why her? Who could want her dead that bad?"

"Any of the Hoopers," he replied. "They're vicious. They'll take any Braeburn they can get. That's the way they work."

"You can't be serious," I snapped. "You're supposed to be a trained scientist. You're supposed to have an advanced education and you aren't even remotely interested in finding out why, of all the cars and trucks belonging to the Braeburns, the killer chose hers? I find that impossible to believe, and I don't believe for one second that it was random chance. Whoever killed her hated her guts. They hated her more than any random Hooper hates any random Braeburn. Any fool should be able to see that."

He studied me closer. "Good point. So why do you think they killed her?"

"You tell me. You know a whole lot more about your family's

dirty laundry than I do. What was she into? For a start, how did she get those needle punctures in her arm? Charlie said you dance with the devil, you pay the price. This is what he meant, isn't it? She was doing drugs."

Jamie grimaced and turned aside to put his tool away. He picked up his phone and started taking close-up pictures of the torn flesh around her neck. "You're a little smarter than I gave you credit for. Yeah, she got mixed up with some bad people this last year. She started spending a lot of time around Rickards Hooper and then she showed up with these. She lost her job as a teacher at the elementary school because she couldn't get to work on time to save her life. She went into a destructive spiral and the Braeburns blamed Rickards."

"Was there any reason to suspect him? Was he known for having access to drugs?"

Jamie shrugged, but he refused to look at me. "I wouldn't know."

I stormed around the table and got into his path. "You know something you're not telling me. This is my life we're talking about here. If I don't find out who *did* kill her, I could be going up for her murder. Do you get that? Whatever you know, you better start talking."

He shot me a fierce glare that made me quail to the roots of my hair. For a second, I thought I might have crossed a line with no way back. He whipped around me and stormed across the morgue.

He halted with his back to me. I should leave. I should get out of here and go find Jada. She would help me.

I drew in a shaky breath, but before I could make my departure, he broke the silence. His voice shook with strain. "There are a lot of things going on in this town that you don't know about."

"How could I possibly know?" I returned. "I just got here yesterday."

He turned around to face me and took off his face shield. His features went through another transformation and his expression changed to something I'd never seen before. "I wasn't going to tell you, but you're right. If you did get pinned with Sophie's murder, it would be my fault for not clearing you when I had the chance."

I frowned at him. "Isn't that what you already tried to do?"

He waved to one side. "Just shut up and listen for once, will you? Don't keep jumping in and interrupting me. Maybe when you hear what I'm about to tell you, you'll understand why I didn't tell Detective Abbott."

I froze. "What is it?"

"I'm only telling you this because you're a witch. If I didn't know you were one, I would never tell you—not in a million years."

Now I was starting to get scared. Did I really want to know? He bowed his head and blew out his cheeks, sighing again. Whatever it was, it must be serious.

He looked down at the ground and mumbled out the side of his mouth as if it hurt him to say the words. "About six months ago, Sophie came to me in confidence. She was pregnant and she wanted me to give her an abortion."

Those words stabbed into my brain with a white-hot needle. An abortion? God, being a doctor must be a real nightmare sometimes, and this woman was his own cousin.

He laced his gloved hands together and then shook them out. "I never told anyone, but these things have a way of getting out somehow. Her brother Eli found out. Maybe she needed to tell someone. I don't know. She and Eli were always real close, so if she was going to tell someone, she would probably tell him. It doesn't matter how he found out, but he did find out and he went ballistic. He immediately started telling the whole Braeburn clan that Rickards Hooper raped Sophie, which was crap because she told me she cared about the father and that was why she didn't want him to find out she was terminating the pregnancy. Whoever the father was, he never knew she was pregnant."

"Rickards could have been the father, though, right?" I asked. "If they spent all that time together, couldn't they have been involved with each other?"

"He couldn't have been the father. It's impossible."

"Nothing is impossible," I countered. "Maybe she was doing it with him to get drugs."

He shook his head. "It's biologically impossible that Rickards Hooper could have been the father."

"What makes you so sure?"

His head shot up and he blurted out, "Because the Hoopers are vampires, okay? There. I said it. The whole Hooper family is one big, swarming, blood-sucking mess of vampires—the whole pack of 'em. Why do you think the Braeburns and the Hoopers hate each other so much?"

I stared at him. For a second, my mind refused to comprehend what he just said. Vampires? My mind flashed to Jada. Every time I'd seen her had been in broad daylight.

"Vampires and bear shifters are reproductively incompatible," Jamie told me. "Sophie might have been involved with Rickards. She might have been nailing him six ways from Sunday. She might have been tramping her body to him in exchange for drugs. She might have been doing a thousand other things with him, but there is no way she got pregnant from him. No way. It's impossible."

I tottered on unsteady legs before I caught myself. I stumbled away and almost fell over the body. "Then someone else fathered her baby."

"Right."

My mind went into a tailspin. "There's no way some kind of mutation didn't happen to allow them to cross-breed?"

He shook his head again. "I examined the fetus afterward. It was curled up in the uterus in bear form, which means that the father was either a bear shifter or human."

I found myself studying Sophie. If only she could tell me what she knew, I might be able to understand what happened to her in the last hours of her life.

"If Eli thought Rickards was responsible for Sophie's downfall," I remarked, "that explains why he attacked Rickards in the alley. What I don't understand is why Eli ran off afterward and didn't come back. Any ideas?"

Jamie picked up his face mask. "I don't claim to understand how his mind works." He stuck the strap on his head and flipped the shield over his face. "I got an autopsy to finish here."

I watched him return to the body. He picked up a pair of tweezers and started peeling the pieces of torn flesh away from her windpipe.

I grimaced down at the gory slash. For the tenth time in a few minutes, I got the distinct impression that whoever killed her must have really hated her—like hated her with a raving passion. They would have to if they killed her like this.

I took another deep breath. "I know you probably don't want to hear this, but maybe Eli killed her. Maybe he found out that she cared about the father. If the father was someone Eli hated, he might have killed her to stop her from being with him."

He didn't look up. "I know what you're thinking, but Sophie wasn't killed by a bear shifter."

I eyed the destroyed flesh of her neck. "You could have fooled me."

"These tears were not made by a bear shifter," he replied. "Trust me, I've seen enough cuts and tears made by bear claws and teeth. These cuts were made by something sharp—something a lot sharper than a bear's bite."

I cocked my head. "Are you sure?"

"Look." He wheeled over a high-powered magnifying glass on a stand. A strong fluorescent light illuminated everything under it. He positioned it over Sophie's neck and held one of the skin flaps underneath it. "See the edges? See the smooth incision along the severed surface? Now look at this."

He went to a filing cabinet in the corner and pulled out some glossy photographs. He held them up next to the magnifying glass. "These are close-up pictures of skin torn by a bear ripping someone's throat out. See the shreds of skin sticking out? That's how the skin tears when the bear bites down and then rips back. These cuts were made by something sharp…and look at the carotid artery. It's cut off clean. The muscle around shows no sign of bruising or crushing injury like you get with a bear's bite."

I leaned back to study him. "You know, it's really kinda creepy how you know so much about this."

He made a face. "I am a bear, honeybunch. Get used to it. I wouldn't be doing my job if I didn't know this stuff."

"So if a bear shifter didn't kill her, who did?"

"Someone who isn't a bear shifter, obviously." He pushed the magnifying glass out of the way and came back with his camera. He held the skin in place with his tweezers while he took pictures of the cuts.

"That narrows the field of suspects, doesn't it?" I remarked. "People keep saying there are hardly any non-shifters in this town."

"Except the vampires," he countered. "Their teeth and claws can make cuts like this."

I squirmed. "Are you sure they're vampires? I saw both Jada and Rickards outside in full sunlight."

He scoffed at me again. "Of course I'm sure. This particular breed of vampires isn't susceptible to sunlight. They can go out at any time of the day or night. It makes them extra dangerous."

My skin crawled thinking about Jada again. She was waiting for me right outside. "I bet it does."

He cast a glance at me over the body. "Sorry to dump all this on you. Like I said, I only told you because you're a witch."

"Well, it doesn't help me clear my name. Any other suspects you can think of?"

"I'm a doctor, not a detective," he countered. "Why don't you use your magic powers to track down the killer? That kind of thing should be easy for you."

I looked away. "For some reason, my spells always have a way of blowing up in my face. Remember the coffee shop incident? That's me trying to be a witch."

His head shot up and his eyes popped. All at once, he burst out laughing. "Oops."

"It isn't funny," I fired back. "Why do you think I had to leave Mount Freeman? I got thrown out of my coven for being a failed witch. They called me a blister. It broke my heart."

He bit back laughter, but he didn't do a very good job of wiping the smirk off his face. "I'm sorry to hear that. My condolences."

"Shut up."

He cracked a grin and bent over the table to hide it. "Okay, so magic is out. It would be super convenient if you could just do a quick séance and find out who the killer is."

I snarled through locked teeth. "I don't ever want to hear the word séance again for the rest of my life."

"So what are you going to do?"

I squared my shoulders. "I'm gonna start work at Eeps's garage tomorrow morning and I'm gonna live happily ever after."

He looked up. "Right after you find out who really killed Sophie, right?"

I lowered my eyes to the body. "Right."

"Atta girl."

I strolled to the door, but I hesitated to walk through it. On the threshold, I glanced back. He was still bent over the body doing something inside the wound in Sophie's throat.

"Jamie?" I ventured.

He didn't look up. "Yeah?"

"You'll tell me if you come up with anything that could help me, won't you? You'll tell me if you find out anything that could help clear my name?"

His eyes shot to my face. "Of course!"

My heart did a flip. "Thanks."

He smiled. Then he went back to work, and I walked out.

CHAPTER EIGHT

I exited the side door in the police station and halted. My vision took a moment to adjust to the brilliant sunshine sparkling over Hurtler's Gulch, but I was in no hurry to go anywhere. I needed to think.

The grocery store still loomed before me like some kind of haunted death ship sailing out of the fog. In exactly twenty minutes, I was supposed to meet Jada over there and share a girl's date of pancakes, confidences, and heart-to-heart talks.

My best friend was a vampire, and I was accused of murdering a drug-addicted bear shifter with a vengeful family and a whole cast of enemies and frenemies. Could my arrival in this nightmare town turn out any worse? I doubted it.

When I pictured myself meeting up with Jada again, a kaleidoscope of images flashed through my mind. First, I walked over there, linked elbows with her, and we both pranced off to the pancake shop where we exchanged BFF friendship bracelets and shared our deepest hopes and insecurities. We promised to have sleepovers at each other's houses and stay best friends forever.

Next, I pictured myself storming over there and demanding an explanation—another one. Why didn't she tell me? Tell me what? That she was a vampire in disguise! I might not have believed it, but if I did, I would have run screaming in the other direction—kinda like I wanted to do right now.

Last of all, I fantasized about sneaking back to Charlie's and not meeting her at all. I imagined dodging behind trees and mailboxes to avoid running into her for the duration of my stay in this lunatic town.

Side by side with all that, another picture came unbidden to my mind. I remembered again the moment when Jamie looked up from his work and I asked if he would help me again. His eyes widened and he said, *Of course!* Then he smiled.

Jada had helped me. She made herself my friend. I had her to thank for steering me to Charlie's and Eeps's.

But she wasn't the only one who helped me. Jamie did a whole lot more and put his reputation on the line to help me with something a lot more important. He stopped Simon and Tony from arresting or shooting me. He gave a statement to Detective Abbott that made it clear I didn't do anything to Sophie in that alley. He also gave me crucial information about the murder case, information that could get him stripped of his medical license and possibly arrested in any regular town.

When I imagined confronting Jada about her being a vampire, I experienced déjà vu. That was twice she'd lied to me by omission. This would be the second time I would be saying the words *Why didn't you tell me?* to her. How many more times would I have to say it if I stayed friends with her?

Jamie never lied to me. Jada said Jamie never lied, but he lied to Detective Abbott. Could I really blame him for that? He couldn't exactly tell Detective Abbott about Sophie's pregnancy and all its countless implications.

I shoved those notions out of my head. Jada was a vampire, but so what? I was a witch, and she didn't know. How long could I keep that under my hat before she came around asking me, *Why didn't you tell me?*

A witch and a vampire. I could think of worse combinations.

She hadn't done anything that would make me not want her as a friend—quite the opposite. She'd done everything to help me.

She also knew as much, if not more, about the Hoopers than Jamie knew about the Braeburns. She might be in a unique position to help me solve the case.

I set off for the grocery store determined to play my cards right. I needed Jada, so why should I push her away just when she'd become most valuable to me?

I turned at the intersection to approach the grocery store and spotted Jada at the entrance. She saw me at the same moment. She rotated around and her face lit up with a welcoming smile. She waved and started walking toward me.

At that moment, two people materialized out of nowhere. Jenny and Patricia slotted in front of me and blocked my path to Jada. They had their backs to her so they didn't see her waiting for me—at least I didn't think they did.

"Just the person we were looking for!" Jenny crowed.

I reared back in surprise. "You were?"

Patricia nodded. "We thought we would find you at the police station, but then we saw you here and decided to pounce."

I did my best not to draw away. "What were you looking for me for?"

Jenny cast a wary glance around and lowered her voice to a confidential murmur. "You better come with us. It's important."

I peeked between them. Jada had retreated to the grocery store entrance, her happy smile gone. She looked back and forth between the two women and inched even farther backward to get away from them.

I didn't want to leave with them. I wanted to get past them and catch up with Jada, but Jenny and Patricia formed an unbreakable wall blocking me.

I made an ineffectual gesture of dismissal. "I can't come with you now—maybe later. I have to be somewhere…"

"You better come now," Patricia growled. "Believe me, there

is nothing you have to do or any place you have to go that is more important than this."

Jenny laid her powerful hand on my arm. "Come on. No excuses."

I shot another glance toward the store entrance. My heart leaped into my mouth, but Jada couldn't help me. She ducked behind a potted plant so the two women wouldn't see her.

Jenny exerted another less-than-subtle push to my arm. I didn't like this at all, but it looked an awful lot like I was going with them, for better or for worse.

I shot another desperate look behind me as I walked away, but this time, I didn't see Jada at all. I was utterly alone with these strange and deadly women.

They sandwiched me between their sturdy frames and marched me across the parking lot. On the other side, Patricia split off and approached a silver-gray sedan parked in an innocuous space. She opened the back door and Jenny steered me into the seat like a convict on my way to execution.

I cowered in the seat while the two women got into the front. Jenny slotted behind the wheel and Patricia took the passenger side. Jenny started the motor and steered out of the parking lot.

I gulped down a lump in my throat. They were going to kill me. I knew it. They were going to take me somewhere secluded, blow my brains out, and leave my headless body in a ditch. Then I remembered. They were bear shifters. They didn't have to use a gun.

The pictures Jamie showed me of torn-out throats drifted before my eyes. In a few minutes, I would be a picture in his files. Soon no one would even remember the idiot pretend-witch who made the mistake of blundering into this town.

Jenny turned onto Main Street and glided out of town. In a moment, she left Hurtler's Gulch and entered the deep, dark, towering woods. She drove onto a winding dirt road that wound into the impenetrable mountains. Yeah, I was dead for sure.

The dense canopy blocked out the sun and cast the forest floor in shadow. Cold sweat broke out on my palms. Could I, in my darkest hour, call up one spell—just one small spell—that would get me out of this?

Even as I thought that, I wasn't completely convinced I could pull it off. What if I screwed that up, too? I might blow up the whole car with myself inside it. I might end up killing myself. That would be just the kind of disaster I would cause.

On and on the road wound with no end. Hours might have passed. I wouldn't know the difference, I was so out of my mind with fear and despair. I scanned the area outside my window. One identical tree trunk after another whispered past the car and still Jenny didn't stop.

Just when I thought my heart would explode from the strain, Jenny turned the wheel. She steered the car to the side of the road and parked. This was it. This was where they would kill me.

Jenny and Patricia turned around simultaneously. They both hooked their strong arms over the bench seat and locked their dark, sharp eyes on me. "We're here to help you, honey," Jenny announced.

I opened and shut my mouth several times trying to understand what she just said. "I—you are?"

Jenny nodded. "Jamie called us from the morgue. He told us to come and find you. He told us all about Detective Abbott accusing you of sabotaging Sophie's car and now we're going to help you."

I blinked at her in stunned disbelief. "How?"

"We're taking you to my grandfather's house," Patricia told me. "Sophie's car is parked in the garage. No one has touched it since the other night when the car broke down in the woods. You're a mechanic. You can check it out and see if you can find out anything about who did it."

My head whipped back and forth as I gaped at them. My

heart nearly lurched out of my chest. "Really? Oh, thank you so much! You guys had me so scared!"

Jenny's granite countenance melted into one of her sunny smiles. "We're here to help you, sweetheart. We want to find out as much as you do who killed Sophie. The Braeburns won't let the wrong person go up for her murder. We have our family honor to protect."

She faced front, started the motor, and started driving again. My heart fluttered, only partly from relief at having dodged a bullet that wasn't coming my way in the first place. Their consideration only raised more questions, though. What would I find, not only on Sophie's car but at the mysterious Braeburn family stronghold in the woods?

Jenny drove a long way. The farther she went, the more I started to wonder whether they really were taking me to a real place or if we would just keep driving around in the woods until the car ran out of gas or we starved to death—whichever came first.

At last, after what seemed like hours but actually was probably only about twenty minutes, she pulled into an open area. Towering, dense woods blocked out the sun. The whole area seemed to be suspended in perpetual shadow.

Buried in this eerie world, she parked in front of an absolutely monstrous log cabin. It was really more of a mansion —or it would have been had it not been constructed of logs. Dripping moss clung to the eaves and the corner angles. The whole thing squatted close to the ground like some kind of massive…well, exactly like some kind of massive bear ready to spring. The whole place breathed bears like you wouldn't believe.

Jenny shut down the motor and an oppressive silence descended over the clearing. It muffled every sound. I kept my breathing shallow, trying to make sure I didn't make any noise that would disturb the ghosts lurking out of sight. This place reminded me of a church.

The two women led the way to a low log building next to

the main house. To get there, we had to walk past the front porch. The windows in the cabin's front wall stared out like eyes following the human stranger who dared to tread on the Braeburn clan's territory.

I scanned the area, tensed at any moment for something to leap out and attack. "Where is everybody?" I whispered.

Patricia waved toward the house. "They're around. Most of them have jobs or something to keep them busy. My granddad is in there somewhere, but you don't have to worry about him."

"Are you sure?" I breathed. "Maybe I should get his permission before I—"

Jenny interrupted me by swinging the garage open. My eye fell on the gleaming, immaculate surface of a cherry-red 1957 Ford Thunderbird. The chrome shone like silver. The whole car had been restored to mint condition and it didn't have a scratch on it. The sight struck me dumb. It was one of the most beautiful vehicles I'd ever seen.

"This is it. Like we said, no one has touched it since the night Sophie was attacked. The Forensics team fingerprinted it and everything, but they didn't find anything. The attacker never touched the car." Jenny snapped around and scowled at me. "Well? Don't you want to check it?"

I hesitated to go inside the garage with that car. It reminded me too strongly of Sophie. I understood her better now, from seeing her car, than I had from seeing her dead body in the alley and at the morgue. This car explained so much about her.

I paced sideways to walk around the car. "If they fingerprinted it, didn't they find out how the attacker sabotaged the car?"

Patricia shook her head. "They said the attacker did something to the onboard computer and they couldn't find any trace of it."

I rolled my eyes. "Lightweights! They could have found out more easily than I could. I don't have the right equipment, but I bet Eeps does. Did you ask him to check the car?"

"He was too busy," Jenny replied, "and then when Sophie turned up murdered and Eli hit the bricks, Eeps said he wouldn't touch the car. He was worried about getting in trouble for tampering with evidence."

I glanced up at her. "Isn't that what I'm about to do?"

She raised her eyebrow at me. "Are you saying you don't want to check the car?"

I mumbled into my collar. "I wasn't saying that." I took a few more steps around to the hood. "This car is amazing. Where did she get it?"

"She bought it from the junkyard. She found it rusted out with no chassis when she was twelve years old. She restored it on the weekends—with Eeps's help, of course. This car was her pride and joy."

"I'll bet it was," I remarked. "Anybody would be proud of an accomplishment like this."

"No one drove it but her," Patricia went on. "She never let anyone touch it. Whoever tampered with it must have known her well enough to know this car would be the perfect place to ambush her."

"Did she have any enemies you can think of?"

Patricia and Jenny exchanged a knowing glance.

I checked between them. "What's wrong? *Did* she have enemies?"

"Only in the last year," Patricia replied. "Before that, she was everybody's little sister. Everybody thought she was the sweetest, prettiest, kindest, most talented girl on the mountain."

I straightened up to confront her. "But not in the last year, you mean. Not since she started running with Rickards Hooper and went down the drain. Isn't that what you mean?"

She nodded down at the ground. "She changed into a skeleton who would do anything to get money for drugs. She stole money out of her siblings' sock drawers. She would pawn her father's last brooch with her mother's picture in it. She even took the family silver out of the dining room cabinet. Nothing was safe." She cast a dejected glance at Jenny before she dared to continue. "People around here really started to hate her."

"Wow," I breathed. "That's really saying something for your family, isn't it?"

"No one hated her as much as they hated Rickards," Jenny snapped. "He was the one who ruined her. He lured her down the path of destruction. She never had a chance before she hooked up with him."

"Yeah, but that doesn't really make sense, either, you know?" I remarked. "Think about it. The Braeburn clan hates the Hoopers with a passion. They avoid the Hoopers like the plague. If we're gonna blame Rickards for luring Sophie to her doom by getting her hooked on drugs, then it follows that he would be the one to approach her. You would think—or I would, at least —that she would be so inured against the Hoopers not to fall for it. She would have pushed him away. She would have hated him too much to have anything to do with him. Wouldn't she?"

Patricia frowned. "What are you saying?"

I held up my hand. "Just roll with me here for a sec. Now let's flip the script and say that she approached *him*."

"She would never do that," Jenny cut in. "She would never have anything to do with one of those scum-sucking bastards."

"But you're telling me that she did have something to do with one of them. She spent quite a bit of time around Rickards one way or the other. One of them approached the other. Either scenario would be extremely out of character for both of them, don't you think?"

Jenny glared at me with a terrible scowl plastered on her face. "Are you going to check the car or not?"

I heaved a sigh and turned around. I came all the way here. I might as well check it even though I didn't have the right equipment to diagnose the computer.

I popped the hood and traced a few wires from the battery to the driver's compartment firewall. I didn't find anything out of the ordinary.

I fiddled a little more with the wiring, but when I still couldn't locate the source of the malfunction, I got suspicious. Maybe there was no malfunction—not that kind, anyway.

I straightened up and went to the driver's door. Then I dropped on the ground and scooted under the car. Jenny leaned down and called to me under the fender. "What are you doing down there?"

"Just checking a few things!" I yelled back. I climbed out and dusted off my hands. "We can go now. I know everything I need to know."

Patricia furrowed her brow at me. "That's it? Don't you have to check the computer?"

"I don't have to because it wasn't a computer problem. No one hacked it, and it definitely wasn't an automotive expert that attacked Sophie. It could have been anybody."

"How do you know that?" Jenny demanded.

Before I could answer, a thunderous voice boomed from behind me. "What in the Sam heck is going on around here?"

I whipped around, my heart leaping into my throat. All three of us did, but the two women relaxed instantly when a giant man with snow-white hair barged around the garage door. He looked like an older version of Charlie, probably because he was one.

Patricia blew out her cheeks. "Granddad! You scared us."

He arched his bushy eyebrows at me. "What are you doing poking around my granddaughter's car? You have no right to interfere with our family business."

Jenny stepped in. "This is Katriona Beaty, Dad. She's the one accused of killing Sophie. Katriona, this is my father, Austin Braeburn."

"If she's the one accused of killing Sophie, then she shouldn't be anywhere near Sophie's car, should she?" the old man roared.

"Jamie told us to bring her. We brought her here to check the car to verify that she didn't kill Sophie. She's here to clear her name."

The old man scowled even deeper. He shot piercing glances at his daughter and granddaughter. "Jamie told you all that?"

"Yes," Jenny breathed. "He saw Katriona at the time of Sophie's death. He gave Detective Abbott a sworn statement that Katriona didn't kill Sophie."

"Oh," the old man barked. He turned his dangerous black eyes on me. "You're the first human ever to set foot on our land. I hope you realize that."

I cowered before his fury. "I'm sure I am, and I am very grateful for your family's help. I'm here to find out who killed Sophie—for your family as much as for myself."

"Jamie says you were found squatting next to her dead body," the old man thundered. "Is that true?"

I looked down at the ground. "Yes, it is."

Another terrible silence followed. Then the old man huffed. "Well? Did you find anything on the car?"

My head shot up. "Huh? Oh. Yes, I did. I found something very—"

He chopped his hand. "Good. Keep at it."

He stormed off and left me standing there with my mouth open. Patricia touched my elbow. Her voice trembled when she murmured in my ear. "Let's get out of here. He's really nice, but he's been in a bad mood ever since Sophie turned bad."

She steered me back to her car. We got in and scampered before another disaster struck.

CHAPTER NINE

Patricia craned around and slung her arm over the front seat while Jenny drove the three of us back to town. "So? What did you find on the car? You said it didn't have a computer problem."

"Those Forensics people really need to get their performance evaluated," I remarked. "They didn't do a very thorough search on that car."

"What do you mean?"

"No one tampered with the car's computer because it doesn't have a computer. The car is too old. I figured that out as soon as I saw it."

"How did they make the car break down, then?" Jenny called over her shoulder. "How did they make it stop right there on that particular curve?"

"They punctured the fuel line—and they left a perfect fingerprint right next to the spot where they did it. Anyone could see it just by looking at it—no magnifying glass required."

Jenny almost drove off the road spinning around to stare at me. "Are you sure?"

"Absolutely sure. All we have to do is get the line fingerprinted and we'll have the attacker in our sights."

"How do we get it fingerprinted?" Patricia asked. "We would have to convince Detective Abbott to come out and go over the car again."

"We don't have to. I pulled the line myself." I drew out the section of fuel line that I removed from Sophie's car. I held it up wrapped in a plastic bag I found on the ground in the garage.

Patricia gaped at it with huge eyes. "You didn't."

"I did." I put it back into my pocket. "Drive to the morgue and we'll get Jamie to do it for us."

"That makes no sense," Jenny countered. "Wouldn't the Forensics team notice that the car was out of gas? I would have expected that to be the first thing they checked."

"They would have, and they would have found out, just like I did, that the car still had a full tank of gas."

"But how?" Patricia asked. "A punctured fuel line would have drained the tank. The car would stop there because it would be out of gas."

"The car has a backup fuel tank," I told her. "They didn't come standard with those cars, so Sophie must have installed it herself—which explains why the attacker didn't know about it. That's another reason to think the attacker was no automotive expert. They knew enough to puncture the fuel line but not enough to notice a spare tank when they were under the car doing it. I'm guessing no one knew the car had a spare tank except Sophie herself and probably Eeps."

"You're not saying Eeps killed her!" Patricia gasped.

"Of course not, dimwit," Jenny countered. "If he knew about the spare tank, he would have punctured that, too. He wouldn't have left the second tank full for her to drive away from the scene." She scowled at me in the rearview mirror. "The second tank is full, isn't it? Please tell me it's still full."

"It is. That's why the Forensics team didn't realize the car ran out of gas."

"So why didn't Sophie just switch to the second tank and

keep driving?" Patricia asked. "Why did she even bother to get out of the car for the attacker to jump her?"

"She was a mechanic," I told her. "She would have noticed that the first tank drained too fast. Like any good mechanic, she would have gotten out of the car to confirm the cause. She would have gotten under the car and seen the puncture in the line. Then, when she climbed out from under the car, whammo! The killer pounces. The killer didn't know or care that the car had a reserve tank. All they wanted to do was get her stopped and out of her car at that particular location and that's what they did."

Patricia shook her head. "It's really low."

"We still don't know that the person who attacked Sophie in the woods is the same person who killed her," Jenny remarked. "It could have been a different person."

"Oh, come off it," Patricia groaned. "Of course it's the same person. Whoever killed her tried once in the woods. When that didn't work, they ambushed her in town."

"It was Rickards," Jenny snarled. "I'd bet anything on that."

"I don't think so," I told her. "When I first saw him next to her body, I thought he was the killer. The more I find out about him, though, the more I think it wasn't him."

"How can you even say that?" Patricia asked. "Of course it was him. He hates the Braeburns. The Hoopers will do anything to harm one of us."

"I don't think so," I persisted. "Like I just said, one of them approached the other. One of them took the first step to get them involved with each other for one reason or another. Whatever reason that was, he would have no reason to kill her— certainly not just out of hatred for the Braeburns and a desire to hurt your clan. That makes no sense. Think about it. Let's say he approached her to get her hooked on drugs so he could get her dependent and milk her for money."

"Bastard!" Jenny growled.

"*If* he did that—and there's no proof he did—then he would

have no reason to kill her or even to put her in danger of getting killed. He would want to keep her alive. Alternatively, if he cared about her, he would want to protect her."

"He didn't care about her," Patricia blurted out. "That's impossible. Hoopers don't care about Braeburns—or anyone else, for that matter. They're vampires. They don't care about anything but themselves."

"If it wasn't him, it must have been one of the Hoopers," Jenny added. "I'd bet anything on that."

I shook my head, but I stopped myself from saying anything. "If you don't think Rickards did it," Patricia demanded, "who do you think *did* kill Sophie?"

I looked out the window. I didn't want to say what I really thought. Whoever got Sophie pregnant was either human or shifter. That ruled out any of the Hoopers as potential father of her child. It might not rule any of them out as her potential killer, but it sure changed the landscape of the case.

If Eli found out his sister got pregnant, it wasn't too much of a leap to think someone else might have found out, too. If the father found out she aborted his child without his permission or even informing him first, he might have gotten mad enough to kill.

I still wasn't ruling out Eli himself as Sophie's killer, but I didn't tell Jenny and Patricia that. Jamie might be the only Braeburn on the planet rational enough even to hear that supposition, much less entertain the possibility.

Patricia sat with her back to the dashboard waiting for me to answer. The minutes ticked past—or were they only seconds? I would have to say something, but what?

I opened my mouth to speak when, out of nowhere, the front windshield exploded in a shower of broken glass. Patricia screamed and whipped around fast. At the same instant, something hit the front seat exactly between the two women. It bored a perfectly round hole in the upholstery and stuffing puffed out of it.

All three of us leaped a foot in the air, but in a fraction of a second, three more blasts echoed out of the woods. The sound came straight through the broken window, now that I was looking at the wide world with nothing blocking my view.

Before I could think twice, another projectile hit the front seat—this time, a good two inches closer to Patricia. Another whistled over the seat and grazed my shoulder before it buried itself in the rear seat.

Patricia whirled right and left shrieking her head off. "Oh, my God! What's going on! What's happening?"

"Can't you see?" I bellowed. "Someone is shooting at us!"

"Where?" she screeched. "Where?"

"Get off the road!" I roared. "Get out of the path of the bullets!"

I lunged across the seat and knocked the wheel out of Jenny's hands as another smattering of gunfire ripped out of the trees ahead. Bullets peppered the hood in a drumming chain of holes.

Something popped in the engine compartment and steam erupted from the motor. It blew the hood back and the sheet metal smashed into the windshield frame. Both women shrieked even louder and Jenny slammed her foot down hard on the gas pedal.

My heart wedged in my throat and my heart hammered fit to burst, but fortunately for us all, I was already half over the driver's seat. I did my best to steer the car off the road with one hand. The hood protected us from continuous gunshots pounding from straight ahead.

I couldn't see where I was going, though, and the car lumbered half onto its side before it bounced bumper-first into a tree. It lurched hard, but I didn't give myself a single second to think twice.

I lunged back in my seat and kicked open the rear passenger door—the one farthest from the road. I hunkered behind the car for protection and crab-walked to the front. I yanked open

Jenny's door, dove inside, and seized her shirt. "Get out of the car! Come on! Hurry!"

I towed her onto the ground. She floundered in dazed confusion, but at least she didn't fight me.

When I lunged back inside for Patricia, she still sat riveted to her seat, jerking right and left and yelling bloody murder. "What's happening? Oh my God! What's going on? What's happening? Oh my God!"

"Come on, Patricia!" I thundered. "You have to get out of the car before they shoot you!"

She didn't respond except to scream even louder. I didn't have time for this. I stabbed my thumb into her seatbelt clip and dragged her out of the car by main strength. She flopped to the ground next to Jenny and screeched louder than ever.

"Who is it?" Jenny bellowed over the noise. "Who would shoot at us like this?"

"How should I know?" I roared. "We have to get out of here before they—"

The noise stopped in a heartbeat. The woods echoed with gut-wrenching silence. I almost wished the killer would start shooting again. At least then I would know where they were.

I stole a peek through the passenger window. The minute I got my head level with the glass, an almighty explosion of gunfire tore the car to smithereens. The windows shattered and the tires burst. The car shuddered with countless concussions.

"What the hell!" Jenny shrieked. "Who could be trying to kill us?"

"Someone who wants to stop us from finding out who killed Sophie, of course."

Jenny and I turned around to stare at Patricia. She had stopped yelling and screaming. She crouched behind the wheel staring at nothing, but she was perfectly lucid—thank God.

"How could they know?" Jenny asked. "The killer couldn't know what we found out about Sophie's car, and anyway, the car doesn't tell us anything about who actually killed her or how or why. It only tells us who tampered with her car, and they couldn't know you brought that fuel line."

The moment she finished speaking, the shooting stopped again. Not a sound disturbed the stillness of the woods—unless you counted the incessant drumming of my heart in my brain. The killer could probably hear it from here.

I immediately dropped into that reverential whisper so as not to wake the sleeping spirits and bring down a hail of lead on us. "It doesn't matter. We have to get out of here. Any ideas?"

Jenny glanced over her shoulder, but there was nothing to see but miles upon miles of empty woods. She didn't have to tell me we were too far away from the Braeburn homestead to expect any help to come from there.

The old man would be back inside sharpening his axe or whatever it was he was doing when I showed up. No one in town knew where we were—except Jamie, and he didn't know we were getting shot at on the side of the road. We were completely alone, alone the way Sophie had been on that night before she died.

"Finley's cabin is only a little way to the west of here," Patricia suggested.

Jenny whipped around to stare at her. "You're right! Why didn't I think of that?"

I scanned the woods. "Where is it?"

"Just over there." Patricia pointed at nothing. "He's a gun nut, too. He's always heavily armed. He'll protect us from… from them."

My mouth said, "Okay, let's go," but I wasn't feeling it, to tell you the truth. I wasn't looking forward to creeping through these woods for an undetermined distance getting shot at by one or more unknown assailants. I wasn't looking forward to it at all —not one tiny little bit.

The three of us huddled behind the car and I drew in a shaky breath to gather my resolve. If this was the only way out, I would do it. I had to.

At that moment, another eruption of gunfire tore the woods apart, but this time, it came from our side. In the time we'd been cowering here discussing our prospects in whispers, the killer must have snuck around the car to attack us unprotected.

In half a second, bullets smashed into the car all around us and another one tore through my sleeve. The three of us jumped out of our skins. Jenny and Patricia screamed, and this time, I swallowed my pride and let myself scream right along with them. I was scared out of my mind and I didn't give a stuff anymore who knew it.

All three of us launched from behind the car at the same moment. I didn't bother to check where I was going. I plowed for the woods in the direction Patricia indicated. I didn't know this Finley she mentioned and I didn't care. Anything was better than staying here getting shot.

Gunshots pursued us into the trees, but we ran too fast and left them behind. In a matter of moments, the dense undergrowth swallowed us and we left the din farther and farther away.

Pure, undiluted adrenaline scorched my veins. I couldn't have slowed down if I tried. Still, Jenny and Patricia outpaced me in no time. They passed me running ahead and beat me to another cabin buried in the forest.

This one really was a log cabin, hardly bigger than a single room. It looked like something out of a history book. A curl of smoke drifted from its chimney, inviting us to rush inside and take refuge from our mysterious enemy.

Patricia broke into the clearing first. She got only halfway to the cabin when, without warning, a figure in a skin-tight bodysuit sprang out from behind the cabin. Black fabric concealed everything except two glittering black eyes.

The person shouldered an automatic rifle and opened fire. Bullets sprayed the clearing and cut Patricia off at the knees. She flipped over and landed on her seat. She tried to scramble away from the assailant, but her legs refused to obey her.

The killer advanced, leveling the gun, but Jenny never broke stride. With a mighty leap, she sprang straight for Patricia and transformed in mid-stride. She changed into a compact brown she-bear bristling all over with spiky fur.

She landed, straddling Patricia, and rounded on the killer, bellowing to shake the Earth. She bared her deadly fangs and peeled her lips back from her teeth.

The killer never missed a beat. Without a moment's hesitation, the attacker fired again. Bullets hit the bear's chest and she staggered sideways. More bullets knocked her hind foot out from under her and her back end slumped to the ground. Jenny tried to rise, but her hind legs were paralyzed.

The killer rounded on me and aimed the gun at my chest. I stopped dead in my tracks, but I couldn't change into a bear to protect myself. Jenny roared again, but she couldn't move. My heart plummeted into my shoes as I watched death stalking me.

The killer advanced and a spark of vindictive pleasure flashed in those dark eyes. The gloved fingers tightened around the trigger. I swallowed hard when, out of the trees behind me, an even bigger bear sailed through the air. It soared past my head and landed on top of the killer.

The creature's sheer size dwarfed anything I'd seen until now. This bear was twice the size of Eli and three times as big as Jenny. It collided with the killer with catastrophic force and toppled the frail body with little effort.

The two bowled along the ground. The bear tumbled free. The moment it got to its feet, the killer rocketed off the ground. The only other time I saw someone jump like that was when Rickards sprang three floors to the roof, but this wasn't Rickards. The person was too short and nowhere near as muscular.

The attacker left the gun lying on the ground and lifted straight off the ground. This person launched at least fifty feet and landed on a branch high above. The attacker gazed down the way Rickards did, but only for an instant. Then they wheeled and took off in a flying streak through the canopy. In a fleeting second, the black figure vanished among the green crowns.

The enormous bear paced back and forth grumbling deep in its chest. Its eyes flicked from one direction to another and it kept arching its back to make the hair stand up along its spine.

I didn't dare go any closer to it. I wanted to run away, but my legs remained frozen to the ground. Jenny howled in pain and rage. She still couldn't stand up.

Patricia twisted around on the ground and propped herself on her elbows. "Finley!" she shrieked. "Finley, are you home? Finley, help us!"

No one answered. The giant bear strode over to the two of them and Patricia laid her hand on its shoulder.

Patricia's voice woke me from my trance. I charged to the cabin and flung the door open, but no one was home. The single room was empty.

I turned around and stopped dead again. A few feet away, Jamie Braeburn knelt next to Jenny and Patricia. The shredded remains of his jeans hung in rags around his hips. Other than that, he was stark naked.

Jenny had shifted, too. She lay half-supported on one side while Jamie worked over both women. I was too busy staring at him in slack-jawed stupidity to understand what he was doing.

He shot a baleful glare over his shoulder at me. "Go inside and bring out the first aid kit, will you? It's under the bed."

He turned his back on me. I had to think hard to make my mind comprehend that he wanted me to do…something.

I ran inside the cabin, fished the first aid kit out from under the bed, and took it back to him. I hesitated to get too near him like this—as if him being half-dressed made him dangerous to me somehow. He just saved our lives. I had to remind myself of that.

He went to work on Jenny with his head down. He ripped packages open and threaded a needle and stripped off tape. He did something that made her scream worse than ever, but in the end, he straightened up and started cleaning up the trash. "That will stop the bleeding until we get back to town. You had a close shave. That's for certain." He looked around at me. "I'll take you three back to town. Start Finley's truck for me, will you, please?"

I took another few seconds to puzzle out what he just said. When I stuck my head into the—you guessed it—rusty old pickup, I discovered that the keys weren't in the ignition. "Where are the keys?" I said, looking in the glove compartment.

"He must have taken them with him," Jamie told me.

"So what do you want me to do? How can you drive back to town now?"

"Hotwire it," he returned. "You're a mechanic. Show us what you can do."

I whirled around to stare at him and found both Jenny and Patricia grinning at me. Jamie cocked his head. "Is there a problem?"

I gulped. "Will Finley be all right with that?"

"If he isn't," Jamie replied, "you can blame it on me. I'll deal with any fallout. This is a medical emergency, so start it."

I put my misgivings aside and got into the cab. I got the decrepit old truck started, no problem. Jamie picked up Jenny and put her in the truck bed. I rushed over and tried to help Patricia, but Jamie came back and took her, too, placing her next to Jenny in the truck bed.

"Let's get out of here," Jamie said. He walked around the truck to the passenger side, but when I didn't move, he cocked his head and frowned at me. "What's your problem?"

I couldn't explain even to myself why I didn't want to get into that truck. I wanted more than anything to get away from anywhere that shooter might come back to and find me. I especially wanted to get away from the cabin before this unseen Finley discovered that I rifled his house and stole his vehicle.

Then again, Jamie told me to do it. That guy seemed to command authority all over Hurtler's Gulch. Whoever the tarnation Finley was, he would probably give me a pass as soon as I dropped Jamie's name.

I still didn't move, though. Jamie strode over and stopped in front of me. He dropped his voice. "What's the matter? Get in the truck. The sooner we get back to town, the safer we'll be."

"I know."

"Then…what are you doing? Is anything wrong?"

"You're…." I looked around at nothing. "You're naked."

His eyes popped. "No, I'm not! I'm…"

He looked down. A dusting of brown-red hair covered his chest. In the handful of times I'd seen him—dressed—since I met him, I never would have imagined he could be this big. His clothes hid his size. He must easily be one of the biggest guys in his clan.

Every chiseled curve of muscle, every crease and crevice, every curl of hair—his whole body screamed bear even though he was a man. He was that monster who leaped out of the woods to stop the killer from shooting at me.

Being alone with him at the morgue or sitting next to him at Charlie's—none of that prepared me for sitting next to him in that truck—like this. Even standing this close to him without his clothes on made my nerves twitch.

He squared his shoulders and jerked his head toward the truck. "Get in. We're leaving."

He marched to the passenger door and got in. For some reason, those words acted on me with an unmistakable command. I headed for the driver's seat and sat behind the wheel. I took a deep breath, pulled the fuel line from my back pocket, and handed it over.

I couldn't look at him. "This is the fuel line from Sophie's car. It has the killer's fingerprint on it."

He rotated the plastic bag in his fingers, but he didn't say anything. I drew in one last shaky breath to steady myself. There. I did it. What happened next was out of my hands.

I put the truck in gear and started driving. Jamie directed me down the long driveway. I didn't see what he did with the fuel line. I put it out of my mind and concentrated on driving in a straight line.

We got back onto the road farther up the mountain from where we got shot at. He didn't speak except to give me his instructions and I didn't try to converse, either. His bare body so close in my personal space made thinking impossible.

I drove around a curve and spotted the wrecked remains of Jenny's car. It sat at a crazy angle smashed against the tree where I drove it. Its broken hood concealed the windshield and driver's compartment.

My heart spasmed when I saw it. I hadn't made much progress toward getting back to town. At least I gave Jamie the fuel line back at Finley's house. At least now I wouldn't forget to do it or something equally moronic like that.

I started to turn to ask him about it, but before I moved half an inch, my heart skipped a beat when that slender figure all in black levitated out of nowhere. The person leaped out of the shadows and landed, standing straight up on the roof of Jenny's car.

Jamie let out a yell to curl the small hairs on the back of my neck, but it was too late. The figure lifted a rocket launcher to their shoulder and fired. The missile corkscrewed up the road and hit Finley's truck in the radiator. A catastrophic explosion shot the truck backward. It tilted over its back end. All four wheels lifted off the ground and it slammed down onto its roof.

CHAPTER TEN

I floundered out of unconsciousness to find myself twisted in knots. I scrambled to untangle myself and stared through the broken remains of the windshield. I had to strain my brain to remember I was in Finley's truck.

The vehicle lay on its roof looking out at the woods. I peered around me, putting the puzzle pieces back together. The truck had fallen pointing the other way. I couldn't see Jenny's car at all, which meant that I couldn't see the shooter, either. Were they still out there?

In answer to my worst fears, another brutal crash hit the truck's underside. The impact skidded the vehicle several feet farther up the road. My mind went into a whirl. Jenny. Patricia. They were in the bed.

I tried to sit up and hit my head on the seat. I was upside down on the ceiling. I pawed my way to the passenger side and dared to touch Jamie's bloody shoulder. "Jamie!" I cried. "Jamie, you have to wake up!"

He groaned and twisted in strange shapes, but he didn't regain consciousness. My heart twisted. This was all on me. I had to do something before…

Another shot pounded the truck. The shooter was out there.

They would keep firing until they killed all four of us—if Jenny and Patricia weren't dead already.

I stole a peek outside. The truck sat at an angle to Jenny's car. That gave me a fraction of an inch of leeway. I scurried out and stuck my head under the truck bed. Jenny and Patricia both lay flat on their stomachs on the ground staring at me with huge eyes. The truck's angle protected them—for the moment, at least.

When I saw them safe and relatively protected, I crawled back to the cab. We weren't going anywhere without Jamie. I didn't care if I had to drag his carcass back to town myself.

I stuck my head in the cab. "Jamie!" My voice cracked from the strain and I wanted to cry. "Jamie, for god's sake, please wake up!"

I jostled his shoulder and he snarled under his breath. "Leave me alone."

My heart leaped. "Jamie! We have to get out of here. You're…" I gulped hard. "You and Jenny and Patricia are all injured. We have to…" I couldn't think of one good thing to do, though.

I was the only one of us who wasn't injured. We didn't have a functioning car between us, and some crackpot was out there shooting at us with a blinkin' rocket launcher. It couldn't possibly get any worse.

It could, though. Oh, yes, in Katriona Beaty's world, everything could always get worse. That was the one thing I learned always to count on.

I inched farther into the cab even though continuous blasts from outside made that prospect dangerous, to say the least. I got as close to Jamie as I could. I forced myself to forget about the fact that he wasn't wearing any clothes.

I took hold of one of his arms which covered his face. When I lifted it down, I had to take a fresh grip on my composure. Blood smeared down his face. "We're getting you out of here, Jamie," I told him, though I didn't believe it.

He cracked a grin that did nothing to quiet my fears. "Sorry, honey. I'm not going anywhere."

He lowered his eyes and I saw his legs. The crash had somehow twisted the driver's compartment. His whole lower body was pinned between the dashboard and the bench seat. He was right. There was no earthly way of getting him out.

"Take Jenny and Patricia back to town," he rasped. "Get help."

"How can I do that?" I raised my eyes to his face and almost burst into tears right then. "I can't go out there with that…that person shooting at us."

Another blow struck the truck to punctuate my point. It jerked the vehicle several inches out of position and he lurched against the steel trapping him. He screamed in pain and the sound set my teeth on edge. I couldn't leave him. No way. Absolutely not.

As soon as the noise died, I checked outside. I still couldn't see the shooter. Where were they? Were they coming closer or were they still standing on top of Jenny's car?

I ducked back in. "We have to get rid of whoever it is. We have to take him out somehow."

"You can't," Jamie croaked. "It's one of the Hoopers. Did you see the way they jumped? Only vampires jump like that. You can't kill him."

"There has to be a way," I returned. "We can't die here."

"Why don't you use your magic?" Jamie asked. "Even if you're not perfect at it, you're still a witch, aren't you?"

I cringed at the word. "Maybe I am and maybe I'm not. You saw me at the coffee shop. All my spells wind up backfiring on me. I would be as likely to blow us up as get rid of the shooter."

"What difference would that make?" Jamie countered. "We're as good as dead anyway."

"You don't understand." I understood perfectly well, though. I didn't want to try it, even without any consequences. I didn't want to fail again.

"Please. Just try," he breathed. "What harm can it do?"

I looked up. His eyes looked the same through all that blood —all except that pained wince twitching his cheek every time he inhaled. He was hurt. He was trapped here with no way out. He might be the biggest, baddest bear shifter on the mountain, but he couldn't get us out of here. I might not be able to, either, but at least I could try.

I turned around and inched toward the driver's window. I stuck my head through and ventured as far as sneaking one eye to the driver's windshield support pillar. Sure enough, the shooter still stood on top of Jenny's car.

I eased my arm forward and pointed my index finger at the stranger. I didn't have a clue who that person was or even if I could do anything. With my luck, the spell would blow back on me, killing me, Jamie, and Jenny and Patricia without touching the shooter at all. That would be so like me.

I took a deep breath. If I was ever going to prove Samantha Vance and her cadre of witch-bitches wrong, now was the time. Even so, her sneering voice still echoed in my brain. *You're a complete failure as a witch.* Would those words remain stamped in my mind for all time? Would I ever get rid of them?

A husky whisper broke in on my thoughts from behind. "You can do it."

If he thought I could do it, maybe I wasn't a complete waste of magical space. Fine, then, I'd give it a shot. I took aim at the shooter and willed my power to flow into my hand.

After several long seconds passed, I wasn't sure it would work at all. Then, suddenly, I felt it. A surge of energy flowed into my hand and out through my finger. A trail of vapor drifted toward the shooter, but it didn't fire. I swirled it in a spiral and willed it to build. I narrowed my eyes at the shooter, focusing, ready to unleash my power on them.

All at once, a tidal wave of unfathomable power rocketed out of my hand. I couldn't control it. It launched out of me with unimaginable speed. Before I could even think to stop it, it blasted toward the shooter and smashed into Jenny's car.

With one colossal boom, it fired the whole car into the air. The vehicle cartwheeled thirty feet, twirled end over end, and sent the shooter spiraling off somewhere. The person made one of their unnatural jumps. The rocket launcher flipped off somewhere unseen and the person vaulted into the canopy again.

The car turned several revolutions and then smashed down on its roof. The impact flattened it in a puddle of twisted steel and broken glass. The gas tank exploded, and a mushroom cloud of red-orange flame plumed out of the undercarriage.

Then everything fell silent.

I stared at the car in stunned shock. The wheels turned in quiet circles. Other than that, nothing moved…anywhere.

I pulled myself together with an effort and withdrew my head into the truck. I turned my attention to Jamie. His bright eyes swam with agony and his lips trembled. Through the muck and gore, his cheeks turned an ashen shade of gray. I had to get him out of here.

I attacked the seatbelt, but that wouldn't do anything to help me when it came to bending the truck frame back into place.

"You did it," he panted. "I knew you could."

I couldn't look at him. "I didn't do anything. I missed."

I had to do something, and this cab was making me feel too helpless. I scooted outside and went around to the bed. Jenny and Patricia still cowered under the truck. "Is it over?" Jenny whispered. "Are they gone?"

"Yeah. They're gone. Come on out. We have to find a way to get you to town. I might need your strength to free Jamie."

I helped both women out, but when I returned to the cab to face the hopeless situation, a screech of tires skidded around the corner. A truck piled with guys peeled into sight along with about twenty cop cars.

What looked like every bear shifter on the mountain jumped

to the ground. Eeps rolled up in his tow truck and he and the cops went to work on Finley's truck with the Jaws of Life.

Three ambulances wedged around the wreck and I lost sight of Jenny and Patricia. I got lost in the tumult. I was all alone among strangers. No one knew what I had done because I hadn't done anything. I might like to take credit for scaring away the shooter, but I knew better. What I had done was nothing but an accident.

All these people—they all belonged to the Braeburn clan. The old man's words came back to me. I was the first human to set foot on this mountain and I would probably be the last. I didn't belong here. I would never belong here.

I should leave Hurtler's Gulch, but in that moment, I realized I didn't want to. A lump stuck in my throat at the thought. In the space of less than twenty-four hours, I'd gotten my life and my heart and my dreams all wound up with these people.

So they were shifters and I was a witch. We were oil and water, but I didn't want to leave. I didn't want to walk away from the possibilities.

Someone touched my shoulder. I looked up to find Charlie at my side. He looked as big and gruff and intimidating as ever. He looked for all the world like a bear shifter. I never thought I'd be glad to see one.

"You better come home," he murmured.

Home. He meant his house. That word passing his lips made it home. It was more a home than anywhere else I'd ever lived. Home. What I wouldn't give to have a home somewhere in the world.

So what if everyone else who lived there were bear shifters, too? So what if I had to talk to them and sit between them and share the food they cooked at mealtimes? I could think of a lot of lives to live worse than that one.

I glanced toward the wreck, but I couldn't see Jamie in the crowds of huge, muscular bodies. The rescue workers and cops and paramedics—all bear shifters—called instructions back and forth. Screeching metal and banging sounded from inside the cab.

I would give anything for just one more glimpse of his face, his eyes. I would give anything for just one indication that he was all right in there, that he was still alive. The truck formed a gargantuan gnarled cage around Jamie. He seemed so small and fragile all of a sudden.

Charlie gripped my arm and pulled me away. He steered me to the truck that brought all the guys from…somewhere. He parked me in the passenger seat and he got behind the wheel.

He turned the ignition and reversed onto the road. No one noticed when he drove me away. Detective Abbott didn't appear to want to take my statement about what happened. Of course not. This was Braeburn country. What happened here was clan business. They would handle it in their own way without any interference from the human law enforcement service.

Charlie parked the truck in front of his house and left the keys in the ignition. I didn't question how its owner would get it back. Anyone would be stupid to touch a truck belonging to the Braeburns. The owner would get it back one way or the other. That didn't concern me.

In a way, every vehicle belonging to any Braeburn belonged to all Braeburns. Any of them could use any vehicle—all except Sophie's car. That was off limits.

I followed Charlie inside. He went to the kitchen where he belonged, and I followed. The whole house was empty without Jenny and Patricia here. They wouldn't be coming home anytime soon, and Jamie wouldn't be showing up for dinner tonight.

I sat down at the table and my shoulders slumped. Everything that happened hit me like a ton of bricks. I still found it hard to believe that it all happened in one day—my first full day in Hurtler's Gulch.

If I didn't walk out that door right now and get on the first bus for Timbuktu, I would be starting work at Eeps's tomorrow morning. So much for taking a day off.

Charlie appeared from somewhere and put a plate in front of me. A large slab of glistening chocolate cake winked up at me. A glorious round scoop of strawberry ice cream melted next to it on the plate.

I looked up to find Charlie smiling down at me. His eyes glistened with a sheen of moisture. "Eat it. You've earned it."

I looked down at the cake. "I didn't do anything."

To my surprise, he sat down on the opposite bench and rested his elbows on his knees. "Do you want to talk about it?"

I stared down at the puddle of pink cream seeping into the lower layer of the cake. I shouldn't say it. I should do anything in the world but say those words out loud. "I'm a witch."

He snorted. "Tell me something I don't know."

My head shot up and my eyes popped. "You know? How could you?"

"Honey, please." He swung off the bench and went back to puttering around his kitchen. "It's written all over your face. Anyone can see just by looking at you. We might be shifters, but we aren't stupid even though everybody likes to think we are. Take Jamie. He's as sharp as a tack. I bet you anything he knew the minute he laid eyes on you."

"Yeah, but…" I didn't tell him about the coffee shop. Them knowing about me being a witch was bad enough. "If you knew all along, how come you're all being so nice to me?"

He shrugged. "Maybe it's because you walked into a family mess that you didn't ask for and we can all see you acting in an upright manner to make sure Sophie gets the justice she deserves. Maybe it's because we get a raw deal from the human world all the time and we don't want to do the same thing to somebody else. Maybe it's because we can understand what it's like to fall and try to pick yourself up again. Either way, it looks like you're stuck with us and we're stuck with you, and you know what that makes us."

"What does it make us?"

He smiled again. "It makes us family, honey. Get used to it."

For some reason unknown to me, my hand migrated to the fork. I intended just to push the melting cream away from the cake, but instead, I somehow nicked the chocolate and put the fork in my mouth to lick it off—just to keep it clean, you understand.

The next minute, I was eating the whole slice. It really did make me feel better. "Charlie?"

He took a cast iron pan out of the cabinet and put it on the stove. "Yep?"

I cocked my head watching him work. "If someone could prove for certain fact that Rickards Hooper didn't kill Sophie and in fact cared about her and wanted to protect her from the killer, would you want to know about it? Do you think any of the Braeburns would want to know, or do you think the vendetta between the two families is more important than the facts?"

His head whipped around and that benevolent compassion in his eyes vaporized in cold fire. "We would want to know—absolutely. I would for certain, and I think I can speak for the rest of the clan, too. We want the truth no matter how uncomfortable it is. We have a code of honor, you know."

I sliced my fork through the ice cream. "I've heard."

"Why?" He fixed me with his most penetrating stare. "Did you find proof of that? Is that what you're saying?"

"No. It's just a suspicion I have."

"Of what?" he asked. "What would make you think that?"

"I don't know. It isn't anything I can put my finger on. It just seems unlikely that someone from the Hooper family and someone from the Braeburn family would spend that kind of time together if they hated each other so much."

"He got her hooked on drugs, didn't he?" Charlie fired back. "She hung out with him because he supplied her."

I shook my head over my cake, but I didn't answer. Too many different thoughts crowded for my attention.

"If you know something, you better spit it out, girl," Charlie barked. "Don't sit on it and leave the rest of us in the dark. That ain't exactly fair, is it?"

"It isn't anything I know for sure—not about Sophie, anyway." I hesitated and then plunged in up to the neck. "I had a sister—a twin, in fact."

Charlie jolted. "Had?"

I nodded again. "She got hooked on drugs. She kept it hidden for three years before she started going down the crapper. She had a boyfriend and he never knew anything about it until close to the end. She overdosed about three weeks before her sixteenth birthday and he was heartbroken. We all were, but no one more than him. He did everything to bring her back from the brink, but by the time anyone found out what was going on, it was too late."

Charlie stopped what he was doing and rotated to face me. He leaned one arm on the stove to study me. "That is one hell of a story, girl. So what are you saying? That Sophie had something going with Rickards? I just can't believe that."

"But you know they were spending large amounts of time together." I waved my fork. "I'm not saying anything about Sophie. I don't know anything about Sophie. I'm just saying she could have been doing drugs for years and no one in your family would have been the wiser. Considering how close your family is, I can see her keeping it strictly under her hat for a long time. She would have been well advanced in her addiction by the time she started showing up around home with sores on her arm and losing her job. That's the kind of thing that happens only at the very end when the addict starts losing control over their life. They can hold it together for years beforehand."

He shook his head and went back to working over the pan. "Well, I won't argue with you. It sounds like you know more about it than any of us do—except maybe Jamie, that is."

"Don't you see?" I persisted. "You all want to blame Rickards for Sophie's addiction when it could have been something else. Maybe she let you believe that because it deflected your attention from something worse—something you would be even less inclined to accept—like maybe they had a relationship going on."

He chopped his hand through the air. "That's impossible. You're talking about a bear shifter getting with a…" He broke it off.

"I already know," I told him. "I know all about the Hoopers being vampires. Jamie told me."

"Then you know there's no way Sophie could have hooked up with him."

"I don't agree with you," I told him. "In fact, I'm starting to think it's the most likely explanation."

"You still haven't explained why you think that," he returned. "Give me one shred of credible proof that supports it —besides the fact that they spent a lot of time together."

I bowed over my cake again. Less than three bites remained. I really fell for that one. "I haven't explained it because I can't. It's just a hunch."

"Then you won't mind if I call it horse-pucky." He took the now empty plate away from me. "Now I suggest you put this murder case out of your mind and go upstairs. Take a shower and then come down for dinner. It looks like it's just you and me tonight."

CHAPTER ELEVEN

I woke up the next morning to that unreal silence blanketing Charlie's house. My first morning there was pretty quiet, too, but not like this. I got cleaned up and dressed and met Charlie in the kitchen. He sat across from me and we ate breakfast together, but we didn't talk.

I ate the eggs and sausage and toast and bacon he put in front of me. When I got up and said, "I better get to work," he shoved a wrapped package in my hands.

I looked down at the white paper. "What's this?"

"It's your lunch. I hope you like BLTs."

I blinked my bangs out of my eyes. "I love them."

"Perfect. Then that's all you'll ever get." He waved toward the door on his way out the back door. "See you tonight. Go get your fingers all greasy and have fun."

He shot me a crazy grin and left. I headed out the front door. My heart flipped walking around the block to Eeps's. I was starting a new job, a new life. After work today, I planned to check at the local clinic and find out where they'd taken Jenny, Patricia, and Jamie. I would visit them and make sure they were okay.

The sun shone on the sidewalk. It was a beautiful day to be alive. Things could be a lot worse.

I turned the corner and walked into the garage. Eeps rolled out from under a random truck and spotted me. "Ah, right on time, I see. You really do have a strong work ethic, don't you? Well, go suit yourself up. I'm not sure we have a jumpsuit in your size, but if you fold back the sleeves and roll up the pant cuffs, you should be fine."

I went to the locker room he indicated, stripped down to my tank top, and got into the smallest jumpsuit I could find. Considering what I'd seen of Eeps and Eli, I wasn't sure they would have one in my size either, but the smallest one fit just right.

I put my sandwich in an empty locker and walked out to the garage. Eeps met me coming from the office. He slapped a set of keys into my hand. "You can get started on that Honda Odyssey parked out front."

I looked over my shoulder. "What's wrong with it?"

"God only knows—maybe nothing. How should I know? Old Man Austin is always griping about something. Half the time there isn't anything wrong with the car that a decent oil change won't fix. Just go over it and see if you can find anything wrong with it. If you can't, rotate the tires and call it good."

He walked away and started tinkering with a big fancy Lexus. A car like that didn't fit with the rest of Hurtler's Gulch, but who was I to argue? I went out to the Odyssey and got behind the wheel. This I could understand.

I turned the motor and drove it around the block. The first time it jounced out of the driveway, a dreadful crunching sound came from the undercarriage. A mind-numbing screech racked the car when I stopped at every intersection.

I drove the car straight back to the shop and put her up on the hoist. I spent the morning replacing the brake shoes, turning the rotors, and bleeding all the lines. Then I changed the shocks.

When I took her down and took her for another spin, she ran as quiet as a purring cat.

I parked the car in the same place and went back inside feeling pleased with myself. I got lost in my work exactly the way I remembered. I was gonna like working here.

Eeps strode out of the garage and accosted me. "You're hired. Go into the office and fill out the application."

I bit back a laugh. "Application? You just said I was hired."

"It's a formality, and when you finish that, do all the other tax declaration paperwork I set out for you. Then come into the staff room and have lunch with me."

By the time I got the paperwork done and retrieved my sandwich, Eeps was sitting at the only table in the staffroom tearing into a giant pizza. "Is that all that skinflint Charlie gave you for lunch? Here. Put some meat on your bones."

I helped myself to a pizza slice. "I like Charlie. He's really nice."

"Of course he is," Eeps fired back. "He's my kid brother, isn't he?"

My head shot up. "Oh, that's right."

"So you knew that?" He waved a hand. "Oh, don't pay any attention to the insults. Those are just our terms of endearment."

"If you say so," I muttered. "I don't even hear sworn enemies talking like that about each other."

He burst into gales of full-throated laughter. He slapped the table and rubbed his sides. "You're funny! I'm gonna enjoy having you around."

"I won't be cracking jokes with my head jammed into a bunch of car chassis," I remarked.

"Too true. I'll have to ply you with pizza, especially if Charlie doesn't kick down with something a little more substantial for your lunch than boring old BLTs. I swear that guy is losing his touch in his old age."

"I like BLTs," I told him. "I wasn't expecting him to supply me with lunch at all. He could have blown me over when he gave it to me."

"Well, you should feel extremely cheated. He usually makes Jenny and Patricia a three-course picnic for lunch and they have sedentary jobs—not like you. You need your carbs by the looks of you."

He stuffed an enormous slice of pizza into his mouth. I eyed him on the side while I bit off a mouthful of my sandwich. For my first day of work, this was turning into a smashing success.

So how come my mind was working overtime coming up with a way to spoil it? "Eeps?"

"Yep?"

"You helped Sophie restore that Thunderbird, didn't you?"

His head whipped around and his eyes flashed. His mouth froze with his tongue jammed into his cheekful of pizza.

All at once, he threw up both hands and slammed them down on the table. "Sweet goodness, don't tell me! They took you up there, didn't they? I wondered what in the tarnation you were doing on Braeburn land yesterday. They took you to see Sophie's car. Admit it."

"I'm not trying to hide it," I returned. "It's no secret."

"Well, you stay away from Sophie's car!" he thundered. "Don't you go poking your nose in where it isn't wanted. You'll only get yourself shot at."

I scoffed. "That's exactly what *did* happen. How do you think Jenny and Patricia and Jamie got hurt yesterday? Anyway, you don't have to warn me off. I already know her car had a double tank and someone punctured the fuel line to make it break down."

He brought his fiery eyes around to glare at me. "If you know all that, then you don't need to ask me about it. We can both pretend none of this has anything to do with either of us and we can go back to working on cars where we belong."

"Do you have any idea why Eli ran away?" I blurted out.

He stared at me. "What does that have to do with anything?"

"He ran away right after his sister was killed. Everybody keeps saying how Eli loved Sophie and would never hurt her, so why did he run off? He worked for you. Maybe it didn't have anything to do with Sophie's death or with him getting in a fight with Rickards Hooper right in front of me. Maybe he got in trouble with you and you fired him for being a young hothead who split work in the middle of the day to pick a fight with an innocent man. I don't know because I don't know Eli from a hole in the ground. That's why I'm asking you."

He dropped his eyes to his pizza. "He didn't get fired. I'm way too busy to fire my only employee. He ran off all by himself and he didn't cut work, either. He had the day off and he didn't come back. I never knew he got in a fight with Rickards until later that day when I heard about Sophie and…and you."

I looked down, too. "Dang. I was really hoping you could tell me something."

"Don't go playing sleuth, all right?" he snapped, but his tone changed to something closer to fatherly concern. "You don't want to get mixed up in this. Just leave it alone."

"Unfortunately, I already am mixed up in it. Detective Abbott wants to pin Sophie's murder on me because he thinks an automotive expert tampered with her car."

"Automotive expert—you!" He guffawed with laughter and startled me out of my seat with the noise. "That's a good one! Come on. Let's get back to work. You can take that Ford Ranger parked by the sign."

He tossed me the keys and stood up. He went back to the shop while I stuffed the rest of my sandwich and another slice of pizza down my throat. He was right. After working all morning, I was ravenous. A few pizzas here and there wouldn't go amiss.

I threw away the paper wrapper and went out to the parking lot. I advanced on the truck, but when I put the key into the door lock, a familiar figure came around the corner to my left.

I rotated and my jaw dropped when I spotted Jamie striding toward me without so much as a limp. His mouth cracked into a crazy grin, but at that moment, a splintering crash hit the truck inches from my head.

Broken glass sprayed out of the window and peppered my cheeks. I whipped back and fell flat on the pavement as gunshots barked down the street. They dotted the fender right next to me.

I screamed in fright and scrambled around the truck to get away from them. I ducked behind the opposite wheel and huddled in a ball as countless bullets pocked the truck all over.

The windshield exploded and Jamie crashed into me, sliding into my hiding place. "You didn't think they would just give up on you, did you? What are you doing, prancing around in broad daylight making yourself such a conspicuous target?"

I rounded on him, shrieking over the noise. "What are you doing here? Aren't you supposed to be in ICU or something?"

He grinned again. "Good afternoon to you, too. It turns out bear shifters have advanced healing abilities, but I didn't come all the way over here to talk about myself. Oh, wait. Yes, I did."

Another smattering of gunfire blasted into the Ranger's engine compartment and punctured the radiator. Water started pouring out of the undercarriage.

I hustled Jamie back around the other way, but this side of the truck didn't offer any better protection from the shooter. I couldn't even see where they were shooting from.

I checked, but we were too far away from the garage. A bullet zinged off the truck bed and made me duck. "Can we not take time right now to exchange pleasantries? We have to get out of here."

He grinned again. "You keep saying that to me, and here I thought you were going to ask me out to dinner."

"Are you insane? I'm penniless and Charlie's your uncle. If you want to have dinner with me, you better ask him."

"I already did." He grabbed my arm. "Come on. I think I know a way we can get out of this."

He pushed me away from the garage. I didn't want to go, but he steered me through a warren of cars toward the next building down the street, which was a commercial kitchen for a catering company.

We huddled behind the Odyssey to gather our courage to cross the side street between the garage and the kitchen. It would leave us exposed with no cover and I didn't see any way the kitchen was going to help us out any better than the garage itself.

I frowned at the building. "Are you sure about this?"

"What choice do we have?" Jamie asked. "It's this or we go from one car after another while she shoots each one to smithereens."

I spun around. "She?"

"Didn't I tell you? I fingerprinted that fuel line you gave me. That's why I came over here to see you. I found out who killed Sophie."

"Well?" I demanded. "Tell me."

"The killer is—" Another belch of gunfire interrupted him. It came from right on top of us. It skittered across the Odyssey's roof and splintered asphalt chips from the pavement near my feet.

I yelled in surprise and hopped away. I bumped into Jamie and he barely caught me before I flattened both of us. He straightened me up as Eeps scuttled in to join us. "So much for that car. That's four hours' worth of work down the hole."

"Do me a big favor, will you?" Jamie thundered at him over the crash of continual shots. "Wheel that big tool chest of yours out here. We'll use it as a shield to get across the street."

"What good will that do?" I hollered. "She's shooting from the roof of the garage—whoever she is. She'll blow us away."

In answer to my words, more bullets pounded into the pavement too close for comfort. This time, all three of us bolted for cover.

Jamie shoved me toward the kitchen. "Go! Run for it!"

I made a dive. The two men ran at my heels, but when another blast of gunfire rained down from above, Eeps and Jamie dove backward to get away.

I got all the way across the gap before I realized they weren't with me. I looked back to see them racing into the garage. I caught one fleeting glimpse of the same black-clad figure standing on the roof.

How could I have failed to notice that she was female? That close-fitting catsuit of hers showed off her lithe, curvy figure. She crammed an automatic rifle into her shoulder and sliced it back and forth to spit bullets in all directions. She covered the whole ground beneath her until nothing was safe.

As I watched, she whipped up her gun and aimed it at me. I turned tail and rabbited into the kitchen, barging right into a huge operation with ten cooks in white coats working over stainless steel tables. They all looked up when I ran in and stared at me with huge eyes.

I swallowed hard. I could see at a glance they didn't have a clue what was going on, but I couldn't stay here. I didn't trust the shooter not to find a way in here, too.

I scuttled through the kitchen, searching everywhere for a back exit out of this place. I pushed through a random door and burst into a warehouse stacked with shelves and pallets and crates of all kinds of stuff.

To my relief, I spotted a rolling cargo door with a small door next to it. A sign called to me, *Loading Dock. Authorized Personnel Only.*

I charged the door, but when I reached it and pushed it open, I hardly dared to look outside. I wedged my eye to the crack and peeked through.

An empty stretch of pavement piled with cardboard boxes led the way beyond the loading dock. A high wooden fence separated the area from houses beyond. I could look over the fence into the sliding glass doors of someone's living room.

My heart hammered into my ribs. I tried to see onto the

roof, but I would have to venture all the way out onto the loading dock for that.

I pulled my head in and wiped my sweaty palms on my jumpsuit. If only Jamie was here, he would know what to do. At least then I wouldn't be facing some murderous shooter alone.

Who could she be? Who would be so intent on killing little old me? Someone who wanted to stop anyone finding out who really killed Sophie, obviously. That was clear. Now she was after Jamie, too. I never should have given him that fuel line. I shouldn't have told anyone about it. If he or anyone else got hurt because of it, I would be the one to blame.

I gathered my courage to go back outside. I had to… What could I do to get out of this? Where in this cockamamie town would I be safe from this murderer?

The police station. I would make a break for the police station. Detective Abbott and all the dozens of bear shifter police officers there would protect me.

I drew in a shaky breath when someone walked through the door I'd just used to enter the warehouse. I stared with my mouth open, watching Jada stroll in. She didn't see me. She went to the nearest shelf, pulled out a box, and started to rifle the contents. She took out a package of pasta, tucked it under her arm, and got ready to leave.

I couldn't let that happen. I grasped at any straw. "Jada! What are you doing here?"

Her head shot up. "Katriona! What are you doing in here?"

"I just asked you the same thing!" I exclaimed. "Don't you know some killer is out there shooting up the whole town?"

Her eyes widened and she looked behind her. "They are? I didn't hear anything."

I frowned at the pasta box in her hand. "What are you doing here, anyway? How did you find me?"

"I work here," she told me. "My dad owns this catering company. I had no idea you were hiding in here." She examined me and then snorted with laughter. "You look like a rat caught in a sewer. You know that?"

My chin fell on my chest. "I bet I do. This is the second day in a row I've gotten caught by that witch."

Her eyebrows jumped up. "Witch? How do you know?"

I waved my hand. "It's a figure of speech. Jamie fingerprinted a piece of evidence from Sophie's murder. He found out the killer is female, but he didn't have time to tell me who it was."

She looked around. "Jamie? Where is he?"

"He's still over at the garage." I stopped and studied her. "You're...you're a Hooper, Jada."

Her mouth fell open. Then she burst out laughing. "What are you talking about? I already told you my last name."

"Don't play it off like it doesn't mean anything," I returned. "You're a vampire."

The smile drained off her face and she got serious. "If you know that much, then you know too much."

She started walking away, but I grabbed her and pulled her back. "You know something about Sophie's murder. You must. You must have some idea if one of your family killed her. She was spending a lot of time with Rickards, wasn't she? Were they involved with each other? Could he have killed her when he got jealous of her?" I stopped short of telling Jada that Sophie had gotten pregnant with an unknown man's child.

Jada gave me a condescending smile. "Rickards didn't kill Sophie Braeburn. He wouldn't get his hands dirty doing something like that."

"How do you know?" I persisted.

"Because he's as gentle as a lamb and helpless as a baby," she returned. "He couldn't hurt a flea."

"But he's a vampire," I pointed out. "He hunts human blood for his survival...and so do you." I scrutinized her, trying to make sense of it all. "You being all buddy-buddy inviting me out to eat pancakes and bagels and stuff and strutting around in broad daylight—was that just part of your act to trick me into thinking you were human like me?" I assumed she'd figured I wouldn't expect a vampire to be out in the sun—and that would have been true, had Jamie not enlightened me.

She smacked her lips and rolled her eyes to the ceiling. "Please, girlfriend. All that stuff about vampires hiding in the dark is a fairytale that humans tell themselves so they don't find out we live among them. You can't believe everything you read in books, you know."

"But you hunt human beings," I continued. "Do you hunt bear shifters, too? Is that why the Braeburns hate you so much—because you hunt them for food? Tell me the truth."

She rounded on me and a hideous grin spread over her lips. Her eyes sparkled and not in a nice way. "You're a lot smarter than I thought you were, Katriona, but I never tried to trick you. I tried to help you, remember? Now I gotta get back to work."

She turned her back on me, but I wasn't about to let my one lifeline slip away. I held her back. "Help me now, Jada. Please. You're the one who keeps saying you want to be my friend. Help me get out of here. I have to get to the police station without the killer shooting me down in the middle of town. Do you know a way I can get out?"

She cocked her head and examined me. "I might, now that you mention it. We just have to…"

She cracked the loading door and checked outside. When no shots rang out, she ventured onto the loading platform.

She craned her head over the side to squint up at the roof. "There isn't anyone there. I think we can make it as far as the grocery store. We can run up this alley and get into the grocery store delivery entrance dock. It's protected on all sides by solid concrete walls. If that doesn't work, I don't know what will."

I tailed her onto the platform. "Okay. I'm willing to give it a try."

She scanned up and down the alley, but silence echoed far and wide. She rounded on me with a crazy grin, seized my hand,

and took off running. I dashed after her trying to keep up. I put my head down and let her do all the steering. If this worked, we would be halfway to the police station before the shooter knew what happened.

We raced up the alley, but after about thirty yards, I happened to look up. I skidded to a halt when I spotted Eeps and Jamie running along Main Street. They veered around Charlie's boardinghouse and dove into a garage next door. Jada kept running and my hand tore out of her grip. She wheeled around to face me. "What's the matter? We're almost there. Don't stop now!"

"Eeps and Jamie are over there!" I vaulted the fence into the yard next to the boardinghouse and charged for the garage.

I wheeled inside with Jada hot on my heels. I nearly collided with Jamie hiding in the shadows. He straightened both arms to prop me up. "There you are! Are you okay?"

"I'm fine," I panted. "I was trying to get to the police station when Jada found me."

I waved at her, but Jamie didn't react the way I expected. In a split second, he lunged in front of me. He slammed his arm into me and knocked me backward toward Eeps. He sprang between me and Jada, baring his teeth and bellowing to shake the Earth.

His face split in half. His jaws extended and his nose stretched into a snout. A flush of brown fur burst out all over his face and his shoulders swelled. He started to change into that monstrous bear I saw in the woods.

In a fraction of an instant, moving so fast I could barely understand what was happening, Jada whipped out a gun, braced her arm, and jammed the barrel into his forehead. She cocked the hammer and her fingers clenched around the trigger. "Don't even think about it, Paddington, unless you want your girlfriend here to be wearing your brains as a dress."

Jamie stopped on a dime. Every trace of bear vanished and he changed all the way back into a man, but he still snarled at her in venomous fury. "You blood-sucking she-devil! I'll kill you! You'll never get away with this."

"On the contrary, my fuzzy brown friend. You and your pals here are the ones who are gonna die. I can't have you blabbing to the whole world what happened in the woods, can I?"

"Jada!" I gasped. "What are you doing? Put the gun away. They're here to help us."

"Don't you get it?" Jamie thundered. "She's the killer! She killed Sophie and she tampered with Sophie's car. She's the one who tried to kill us in the woods. I found her fingerprint on the fuel line. That's what I was about to tell you when she started shooting. Don't you know that by now? This bitch is NOT your friend."

I turned around to stare at Jada. "Jada! You couldn't!"

Her lips curled off her teeth. All at once, she looked exactly like a bloodthirsty killer on the hunt. She didn't care about me. She never cared about anyone but herself. "You stupid, bumbling witch! I spotted your stupid ass the minute you set foot in this town. Why do you think I set you up to take the fall for Sophie's death? You were the perfect target."

"You!" I gasped. "You set me up?"

"Who better than you? Everyone in this town hates witches. I told you to go around the block to Eeps's garage and ask for a job to get you in position. I waited until you got close enough to Rickards and Sophie."

"But that means…" I stammered. "That means you set Rickards up, too. Why would you cast suspicion on your own brother?"

She narrowed her black eyes to slits and her teeth gnashed. "The Hoopers don't mix with the Braeburns. I warned him when he started getting all mushy about her. Do you know that idiot actually thought he and Sophie were going to bring peace to our clans? He thought they were gonna be some kind of modern-day Romeo and Juliet. Can you believe that crap? I told him it would never happen and I made sure it didn't."

"You bitch!" Jamie hissed. "You'll fry for this."

She laughed in his face—a high, vindictive laugh with no warmth in it. "You stupid pig. Who do you think you're talking to? No one can touch me. Do you really think your pathetic little justice system can do anything to me? You three will go down and no one will find out anything about me. Even if, by some chance, someone did arrest me or put me in jail, I could get out of it whenever I want. No one can touch our kind. You should know that."

My skin crawled listening to her. She was right. No one could harm a vampire. They were immortal—or as good as. Besides, she was the one with the gun pointed at us.

Eeps barged forward. "I'll show you hurt. I'll break you in half."

He made a grab for her, but Jamie caught him and wrestled Eeps back. "Don't!"

Jada laughed even louder. "Listen to your nephew, bullethead. Now we'll just take a walk right over there in the corner and then we'll…"

She jammed the gun into Jamie's ribs. When he didn't obey her right away, she snatched his elbow. He tried to struggle, but she overpowered him easily.

She marched the three of us into the corner. "Turn around and face the wall."

I did as she said, expecting a bullet to put me out of my misery any second now. To my surprise, she draped a heavy chain around us, cinched it tight, and locked it with a combination lock.

She grabbed Eeps by the back of the neck and propelled us back the other way to the door where we entered this garage. It was a lot harder to walk chained up with two massive bear shifters. Jada didn't help by poking her gun into us one after the other and barking threats.

We stopped at the threshold. "Now what?" I asked. "What are you going to do with us?"

"Shut up," she snapped. "You're not here to think."

"You won't get away with this," Eeps snarled.

"Who's gonna stop me—you?" Jada snorted and stuffed her gun into her belt. "Now keep still. I would hate for you to fall to your deaths."

Without so much as a strain, she picked up all three of us in one big bundle. She heaved us onto her shoulder like she was carrying a feather pillow, chain and all.

The moment she got us into position, she jumped into the air. She jumped exactly the way she jumped in the woods yesterday. She took off and soared into the air.

The next minute, she sprang in wild leaps from one roof to the next, covering the whole town in a few steps. She jumped to the ground and zoomed into the trees. Our weight didn't slow her down at all. She buried herself in the trees and the town vanished.

CHAPTER TWELVE

Jada set us down in a wrecking lot that must have been a hundred miles out of Hurtler's Gulch. She dumped us next to a pile of rotting car parts, making no attempt to put us down gently.

I yelled when Jamie and Eeps landed on top of me, but none of us could do anything with that chain holding us together.

Jada kicked Jamie hard in the thigh. "Keep still and keep your mouths shut. Don't make me tell you again or it will be worse for you."

"How could it possibly be worse for us?" he demanded. "You're gonna kill us anyway."

"Shut up, I said!" she roared. She crammed the gun into his face. "Don't give me any reason to use this."

"Use it," he countered. "What difference does it make? What are you gonna do—bleed us first? That would be just like you."

She bared her horrible fangs. I couldn't see them as anything else right now. She gave a menacing laugh. "Right again, pig. Are you volunteering to go first?"

Jamie pulled his head in. Jada got ready to say something else, but I couldn't stand to listen to her threats anymore. "I can't believe I tried to be your friend."

She rounded on me with that nauseating grin. "You're as stupid as the rest. That's what made you such a perfect target."

"Don't you think it will spoil the effect if we all turn up dead?" Jamie asked. "You won't be able to pin the murder on Katriona if she's dead. Everyone will know you did it."

"What do I care?" Jada straightened up, still grinning like a fiend. She swept her gun over us without really aiming. "I'll be long gone. I always wanted to get out of this pissant town and now's my chance. I'll go to New York or L.A. where vampires really know how to live, and I'll never have to taste your filthy shifter blood again. I'll be feasting on real human blood for the rest of my days."

"But not before you taste ours, right?" Jamie countered. "Don't forget about that."

Jada ran her slimy tongue over her lips, leering at him. "Revenge is a dish best served cold, isn't it?"

"What revenge?" I asked. "You didn't do it out of revenge and you aren't killing us out of revenge, either."

She shrugged and turned away. "It doesn't matter. I always wanted to use that line and now I have."

She strode away and rounded one of the piles of rusting car bodies. We lost sight of her and my heart sank. "We're screwed. We can't beat her. She's too strong."

"Use your magic," Jamie whispered in my ear. "See if you can break this lock."

I looked up to stare at him. "You're kidding, right? Even if I could break it, we would be just as screwed and we would only tip her off that we're trying to escape. It's too risky."

"Just try it," he breathed. "We have nothing to lose— nothing at all."

My insides seized. He was right about that last part. If Jada caught us running for those trees, we wouldn't be any more dead than if we sat here and waited for her to finish us off one after the other.

I turned my attention to the lock. How bad did it have to

get before I realized I was hopeless? *You're not a witch. You're a blunderer. You're a blister. You're a boil on the buttocks of magic.*

I did my best to push those words out of my mind, but they wouldn't leave me alone. I botched every spell I ever tried. I pretended that wasn't the case because I didn't want them to throw me out of the coven, but it was all true.

If I botched this…what? I would be dead. Eeps and Jamie would be dead, too.

I traced my forefinger over the metal and summoned up my power. Through the vapors, I explored the mechanism inside the lock. I gripped the tumblers and started to turn them when footsteps made me yank my hand back in a hurry.

Jada barged around the cars and made straight for us. Without so much as a by your leave, she stuffed the gun into Jamie's face while she turned the number wheels on the lock. She kept her hand over the tumblers so I couldn't see the combination.

She whipped off the chain and laid hold of Eeps. "You first, geezer." She hauled him out and held him with one hand while she wrapped the chains around me and Jamie again. She locked them in place and yanked Eeps away.

Eeps cast one hopeless glance back at us. The next minute, he vanished around the cars with Jada's gun jammed into his ribs.

"Do something, for Pete's sake!" Jamie whispered to me.

"Like what?" I murmured back. "My magic never works."

"Stop with the pity party, Katriona!" he hissed. "You blew up that car yesterday. Can't you do something like that now?"

"That was a mistake, you fool!" I screamed in a desperate whisper. "I was aiming for Jada and I hit the car. I flub every spell I try. You've seen that yourself."

"Who cares if you miss as long as you get the job done?"

"I can't do anything against Jada," I cried. "She's a vampire. I never learned any magic for taking one of them out because there is no magic for taking them out! She's invincible."

He leaned his face close to mine and hissed through gritted teeth. "You have to do something! I don't know what and I don't freakin' care! She's gonna kill Eeps in a matter of seconds. You know that, don't you? For the love of god, do something! It doesn't matter what."

My mind went haywire. I couldn't let Eeps die. I bent over the lock again. No pressure. Only a man's life hanging in the balance. Nothing to worry about.

I extended my power into the lock one more time when a spine-chilling shriek echoed through the lot. My hair stood on end and Jamie and I both stared to the place where the sound came from.

Jamie whipped around. "Hurry! Please! Just do something. I'll do what I can, but you have to use your magic."

"I can't!" I shrieked. "I'm not a witch! I'm an imposter."

The look on his face made me feel a thousand times worse than anything he could have said out loud. I'd failed him. I failed myself and Eeps and everyone else, but no one worse than him. That hurt more than everything.

I bowed my head over the lock. If I was going to die anyway, if Eeps and Jamie were going to die, too, then I had nothing to lose. If I screwed it all up, what difference did it make?

I took a magical grip on the tumblers and rotated them into position. The metal hook popped. The lock fell open.

Jamie grabbed the chains and whipped them off. "Come on! Hurry!"

He hurled the chains aside and we both took off running. I struggled to breathe, but my lungs refused to function. What would we find when we rounded those cars?

We both slipped in the soft grass and my heart leaped into my mouth. Jada held Eeps by the hair with one hand. The fingers of her other hand clamped around his neck. She reared back with her spiked fangs bared to strike at his jugular vein.

Jamie launched at her, bellowing to high heaven. He rocketed off the ground, shifting in midair, but he was too far away. In half a second, Jada would bite Eeps's neck and it would be all over.

Without thinking, I shot out my hand and pointed at Jada. I wasn't thinking or even trying, but a scorching-hot jet of fire poured out of my finger. It zinged across the yard and sliced Jada across the wrist.

She yanked her hand back and Eeps dropped flat on his back. In a split second, he bounced up, shifting in a heartbeat. He levitated off the ground, splitting his back in half. His shoulders exploded to a huge size and he changed into a raving, rampaging bear.

He and Jamie closed around Jada. They pounced on her, roaring in rage. They buried her under their monstrous bodies, but in half a second, she hurled them off with the slightest flick of her arms.

The two bears sailed dozens of feet and landed hard a safe distance away. Jada reacted quicker than I thought. She jumped into the air shrieking a high-pitched feral howl that set my teeth on edge.

She charged Jamie with her fangs exposed to rip and shred. Her fingers extended to claws and her eyes flashed unearthly fire.

My blood ran cold watching her arc toward the prostrate bear. If she landed on him, she would kill him for sure. He couldn't fight her. No one could fight her. She was undead. No one could kill her.

I had to stop her. I held up my hand. I had no idea what I would do, but something inside me said, *No.* The same heat poured from my fingertips and hit her. The power propelled her away, but only a short distance.

I had no idea what I was doing. I wasn't trying at all. It just happened. She landed in a crouch a short distance from Jamie and locked her venomous eyes on me. She bared her teeth. Here it comes. She would kill me first and then she would finish off Eeps and Jamie.

I traced my fingertip in the air. I didn't know any spells

against vampires—certainly none strong enough to stop Jada—so I used the only spell I did know: the Smithersley Incantation.

I practiced it so many times in recent weeks that I still had most of it committed to memory. I went through the sequence and watched the silvery vapor form faces and pictures. They rotated around Jada.

She bared her teeth at the apparitions. She screeched and howled at them, but that didn't stop them coming closer. I got so engrossed in watching her reaction that I forgot what I was doing. I repeated the incantation automatically.

The apparitions became stronger and more distinct. They circled around Jada and their beautiful faces changed to skeletal ghouls. Their yawning mouths grimaced at her and they wrapped their ghostly arms around her.

She slashed her claws at them. Her screams echoed through the woods louder than ever. The sound alone would wake the dead.

She couldn't hurt them with her teeth and claws, though. More apparitions floated out of the fabric of reality, surrounding her in a veil of white. She stared one way and then the other with terrified, confused, frantic eyes. Her expression changed to one of abject terror.

I realized from a distance that I still had my arm outstretched toward her. My finger still copied the symbols in midair without me even thinking about it. I watched in fascination as Jada pinwheeled her arms trying to fight off those apparitions.

All at once, she charged forward. She rushed me, broke through the circle of ghosts, and stopped. Her vision cleared now that the apparitions no longer surrounded her. Her gaze rested on me and that cold, deadly fury congealed in her features.

This was the end. She would attack me and there wasn't any magic on Planet Earth that could stop her from doing her worst. I relaxed into the inevitable when, out of the clear blue sky, a tremendous roar split the stillness. A lean figure dropped out of the trees and landed right on top of Jada.

I jolted back and stared at Rickards attacking Jada with tooth and claw. My heart pounded in my neck, but I was far enough away not to be in any danger from either of them.

Jada tried to fight him, but he overpowered her in seconds. He snatched her off the ground, twirled her around his head, and slammed her down on the ground. Eeps and Jamie inched out of the way, too, but Rickards concentrated all his ire on Jada.

She hit the ground with catastrophic force. Rickards towered over her with his face transformed into a mask of grim determination. He reared back and raised his foot. She lunged to get off the ground, but he kicked down with all his might and planted his foot in the center of her chest.

The sheer velocity of his kick nailed her to the ground. She let out a sickening scream, but he only gritted his teeth and ground his foot into her torso with brutal fury. He crushed her under his heel. Then, with unholy speed, he dove for her throat. He dropped on his knees and buried his fangs in her neck.

I shuddered watching them. Rickards crouched tense and deadly over Jada. She flailed her arms and legs, but in a second, her limbs flopped onto the grass. A quiver went through her, but he didn't relax in the slightest. He didn't let go until she exploded in a cloud of dust and vaporized to nothing.

CHAPTER THIRTEEN

Rickards drew himself up and his shoulders shook with strain. He bowed his head and stared down at the place where Jada wasn't anymore. I didn't want to go near him, but he just saved our lives from one of his own kind.

Eeps and Jamie pulled themselves to their feet and I dared to take a step forward. Rickards kept drawing broken gasps every time he breathed. I put out my hand, but I hesitated to touch him. I opened my mouth more than once before I got my voice to work. "Thanks."

He didn't look up, just furrowed his eyes at the ground. Not one drop of blood remained of Jada. He didn't have any blood on his face from biting her, either. "Killing Jada won't bring Sophie back. I wish it would. It doesn't change anything. It doesn't make anything better."

"It does make something better," Jamie interjected. He migrated to Rickards's side and he didn't hesitate at all to lay his hand on the young vampire's shoulder. "You saved our lives. That's one step in the right direction toward peace between our clans."

Rickards still didn't look up. "I didn't get her pregnant. You have to know that."

Jamie sighed. "I do know it. I know you never did anything to hurt Sophie. Jada framed you to make it look like you did. She killed Sophie to stop you from making peace between us, but you did it anyway."

"Do you have any idea who got her pregnant?" I asked.

"His name is Cory. He lives over in Mount Freeman. He's a hard-core drug dealer. He promised to make Sophie one of his distributors if she did it with him. She would have gotten her own drugs for free in exchange for selling a certain amount." He huffed under his breath and shook his head at the ground. "I tried to stop her. I even said I would break up with her if she did it with him, but she didn't listen. She wouldn't listen to a word I said. Toward the end, I don't think she even knew I existed."

My stomach twisted in knots listening to this. It brought back too many memories.

"You're the one she cared about," Jamie told him. "You were the one she didn't want to know just how low she sank at the end. She wanted to protect you from herself."

"Well, it didn't work," he muttered. "She didn't protect me from this, did she? She's gone and I have to live with that. I have to live in this rotten old world without her. She didn't protect me from that."

Without thinking, I put out my hand and touched his arm. He actually felt human. I wasn't expecting that. "It isn't Sophie's fault she got killed. Jada killed her for loving you. Her addiction didn't cause her death."

He didn't seem to hear me. "Now I have to go home and tell the old man what I did. He'll probably attack me and try to kill me. He doesn't know about Sophie and me." He cast a wary glance around the forest. "None of them knows."

"Don't leave, Rickards," Jamie urged. "Don't leave Hurtler's Gulch. We need vampires like you. You're the only one who wants peace."

Rickards only shook his head. "That's exactly why they won't let me stay. If the old man doesn't kill me, he'll drive me out. He might be merciful and send me to some other branch of the family hoping they'll straighten me out, but they'll never get Sophie out of my heart. No one will ever be able to do that." He shot a harsh glare at Jamie. "Thanks, man. Thanks for being there for Sophie at the end. I'll always owe you for that."

Jamie only shrugged. "I was just doing my job."

"I better go," Rickards muttered. "The sooner I get this over with, the better."

He made one of those insane jumps, vaulting into the treetops and vanishing in a breath of wind. Eeps, Jamie, and I watched him go. Jamie sighed again. "Well, that's it. I hope he sticks around. I really do. He's one of a kind."

"He's a good kid," Eeps rumbled. "I never thought I would live to say that about any of the Hoopers, but he's all right."

Jamie touched my elbow. "Come on, girl. Let's get you back to town where you belong. If I'm not mistaken, there's a Ford Ranger at the garage with your name on it."

I couldn't laugh. I kept scanning the trees hoping to catch one last glimpse of Rickards even though I knew he was gone. I really wished he would stick around town, too, but under the circumstances, I couldn't be sure I would ever see him again in this lifetime.

What a shame that the one decent vampire in this town would have to go on the run or maybe face death at the hands of his own relatives. It wasn't right, but there was nothing I could do to help Rickards, much as I'd like to.

I turned away to follow Eeps and Jamie out of the lot. "What will we tell Detective Abbott about the murder case?"

"Nothing," Jamie replied. "Don't tell him anything. I gave him the fuel line and the fingerprint, so you should be all clear. He'll know Jada tampered with Sophie's car. Other than that, it's a cold case as far as I can see. They'll put it in the cold case files and it will stay there. Detective Abbott and the rest of the human world will never find out what happened here."

"That's too bad," I remarked. "It's too bad Rickards won't get the credit he deserves for saving us."

"Oh, he will," Eeps chimed in. "The Braeburns will never forget. You can bet on that. In a few hours, everyone will know exactly what he's made of. He'll have friends in this town for life even if his family turns against him."

We stepped out of the lot, but only solid woods surrounded us on all sides. "So how are we going to get back to town? It must be at least a hundred miles."

"Not that far. Get on. We'll be home in time for dinner." Jamie dropped onto his hands and knees and transformed into a bear. Fur sprouted all over his skin and his huge head lowered between his giant shoulders.

I stared at him. Get on? Was I really supposed to ride on… on that? He rumbled low in his chest and lowered himself onto the ground. He still towered above my shoulder, but what other option did I have?

Eeps shifted, too. That left me little choice. I took two handfuls of Jamie's fur and clambered onto his back. I straddled his shoulders and held on for dear life.

The two bears took off at a fast run. I flattened myself against Jamie's back, focusing all my strength on holding on. The wind whistled through my hair and stung my eyes. Miles of woods passed under his feet and still he ran.

I lost track of time until he slowed to a trot. I sat up and caught my breath again as he and Eeps loped into the clearing at the Braeburn family stronghold.

Jamie stopped at the front porch and I slid to the ground. Eeps and Jamie both shifted, but now that all three of us were back in human form, the house and the garage and the surroundings never seemed quieter. A pall hung over the homestead.

Jamie bumped my elbow. "You go back to town. Eeps will give you a ride home."

I spun around. "What about you?"

Before he could answer, the front door slammed open and Old Man Austin Braeburn stormed out. "What the devil is going on around here? How many times do I have to tell you kids not to bring humans around this house? Don't you know she's dangerous to our kind?"

Jamie looked up at him. Then he turned back to me. "Go on," he breathed. "I'll handle this."

"Are you sure?" I asked. "I could stay and…"

He shook his head, but his face lit up in a brilliant smile. "I'll explain everything to him. You have nothing to worry about."

Where had I heard those words before? I knew enough by now to trust him at his word. I swallowed hard. "When will I see you again?"

He grinned even wider. "Charlie invited me for dinner. Go with Eeps now. I'll see you later."

I backed away. He watched until Eeps led me to a different garage. A rusty old pickup sat parked inside. Eeps got behind the wheel and I took the passenger seat. The last glimpse I had of Jamie was of him escorting Old Man Austin back inside the house. God only knew what Jamie would tell him. Probably the truth.

Eeps started the motor and drove down the mountain. This time, no mysterious masked killers jumped out to gun me down. The truck trundled into town. Hurtler's Gulch looked different all over again. It looked different from when I first got off the bus. It even looked different from when I first found out it was infested with shifters and vampires.

For some reason I couldn't explain, it actually looked more normal, now that I knew so much about it. The majority of people walking around on the streets were shifters, but that didn't bother me anymore. It seemed natural.

The vampires weren't so obvious, but even they fit with the overall pattern. Maybe, by some miracle, Rickards wasn't the only one who wanted to end this blood feud. Maybe one of these days the people who wanted peace would succeed in getting it.

That was the strangest thing. All these curious creatures were really just people like me. Rickards. Jamie. Charlie. Jenny. The oddities of the paranormal world I would have shunned less than a week ago—now they were normal to me. They were my friends —my family, as Charlie said.

Eeps parked in front of Charlie's boardinghouse, but he kept the motor running. "You better go inside and get yourself cleaned up for dinner. You know what Charlie is like if you're late. I gotta drive over to the shop and sweep up a mountain of broken glass."

I whipped around to find him smiling at me. "I could come and help you. You don't have to do it all yourself."

"You've done enough for one day. Go inside and I'll see you bright and early for work tomorrow morning. Don't be late."

His eyes sparkled and his cheeks flushed with color smiling at me. That face told me all I needed to know. "Okay. Just don't touch that truck. She's all mine."

He put the pickup in gear. "Oh, I won't touch your truck. I wouldn't dream of it."

I stepped out onto the sidewalk and he waved to me as he drove away. Now came the hard part. I hauled my exhausted carcass up the steps and stepped into the house.

I stopped in the front hall. Voices came from the kitchen all mixed up with the slamming of pots and pans. Charlie's big, rolling laugh echoed through the house. This place never felt more like home.

I never had a home before—not like this. I only just realized that. This was my home and this was my family. Don't ask me how it happened, but it really was true. I never would have picked a bunch of bear shifters to be my family, but it seemed to work out that way anyway.

A female voice came from the kitchen. I snuck down the hall

and listened. Jenny. Patricia was in there, too. They were talking to some other man whose voice I didn't recognize.

I peeked around the corner and gulped. Eli. He sat in the corner talking to the other three like he belonged there.

I yanked my head back, struggling to still my fluttering heart. Why did I go into palpitations finding him here? Wasn't he related to the rest of the Braeburn clan?

He didn't kill Sophie. He didn't have anything to do with Sophie's death. He found Rickards next to her body and he thought Rickards killed her. Anybody could understand that. He must have gone on the run because he was worried he would get in trouble.

Either way, he wouldn't be here now unless everything was cool between him and his family. I was the only one who wasn't cool with it.

I staggered to the stairs and hustled to my bedroom. I shut the door and sank down on the bed. In a few minutes, I would go down to dinner. Jamie would show up and maybe Eeps. We would all talk and laugh and relax and share one of the best meals on the planet. What could be wrong with that?

I looked down at my hands in my lap. The fingers didn't seem to belong to me. None of this seemed to belong to me. My shattered brain couldn't conceive that all the terror and tension and danger of the last few days was all over.

Here I was. I was living in Hurtler's Gulch now. I was part of this community for better or for worse. Part of me wanted to cry and part of me wanted to laugh. I didn't know what to do.

A loud voice drifted up the stairs and woke me from my trance. Was that Charlie calling me to dinner?

I hurried to the bathroom and splashed water on my face. I got myself as together as I could and went back down.

"Here she is!" Charlie boomed when I walked into the kitchen. "You're right on time." He waved to the table. "Eli Braeburn, this is Katriona Beaty, our newest automotive genius."

Everybody laughed and Eli stood up to shake my hand. He

dipped his chin, and the faintest trace of a smile twitched his lips. "We've met."

I blushed. "Yeah."

We sat down and I turned my attention to Jenny and Patricia. "Are you two all healed up, too?"

"Fit as a fiddle," Jenny replied. "Nothing to worry about. You, on the other hand, look like you've seen a ghost."

I shivered. "I guess I have."

"Jamie's late," Charlie snarled. "That boy deserves a hiding for this."

"He got hung up at the homestead," I told him. "Old Man Austin got bent when Eeps and Jamie turned up with me again, so Jamie stayed behind to explain the situation to him."

Charlie's head jerked around and he scowled at me. "What situation?"

I lowered my eyes and screwed my thumbnail into the tabletop. "I'm sure Jamie will tell you all about it when he gets here."

"Tell us now," Jenny interjected. "Did something happen?"

I shrugged. "We busted Sophie's killer."

Everyone froze staring at me, no one more than Eli. "Who was it?" Charlie demanded. "Don't leave us in suspense."

"It was Rickards, wasn't it?" Jenny snarled. "I knew it all along.

"It wasn't Rickards," I muttered. "It was Jada. Jada Hooper."

"Don't tell me *you* caught her," Charlie fired back. "What did you do—hex her or something?"

"I didn't do anything," I mumbled. "Rickards was the one who stopped her."

"Rickards!" Jenny exploded. "I don't believe it."

"He killed her."

The whole kitchen erupted in talk. They fired questions and protests and arguments all at the same time about how what I said must be impossible. I got so confused and flustered I couldn't make out what anyone was saying.

Charlie came over and propped his huge arms on the table. He yelled down at me, trying to make himself heard over the noise. I prepared myself to run from the room when Jamie walked in.

"What the holy heck is going on here?" He sounded exactly like the old man when he talked like that.

Everyone rounded on him at once. While they pelted him with questions and exclamations, who should roll through the door but Eeps himself.

I huddled low in my seat while Eeps and Jamie explained everything to everybody. They told and retold the whole story from front to back while I cringed and pretended to be invisible.

In the end, Charlie leveled me with a direct stare. He whispered under his breath. "I don't believe it!"

Jamie pulled up a section of bench next to me. "Believe it. It's all true. You folks spread the word through town that Rickards Hooper is all right. If he stays in town, he's under the Braeburns' protection from now on."

"Did Granddad say that?" Patricia asked.

"I said it," Jamie fired back. "I told Granddad and I'm telling you. Anybody who lays a finger on Rickards Hooper will have to tangle with me."

"And me," Eeps snarled.

A chill descended over the room and everyone fell silent. After a tense silence, Charlie hmphed and went back to the stove. "All right. If that's the way you feel about it."

He took an enormous tray of spareribs out of the oven and set it in the middle of the table, along with bowls of salad and potato salad, steamy hot white bread and butter, green beans, beets, and roasted carrots.

Arms and legs started flying in all directions and conversation restarted. Jamie leaned across me to pick up the potato salad. "Have you been introduced to Eli—properly introduced, I mean?"

I blushed again and caught Eli looking up at me. "Yeah. I have."

"My granddad wants me to bring you around the homestead so you can be properly introduced to him, too," Jamie told me.

I froze. "He does?"

"I already introduced her," Jenny interjected.

Jamie shook his head. "He says that wasn't a proper invitation. He wants you to come over for dinner one of these evenings so you two can get acquainted."

I stared at him, trying to get my parched throat to function. "But I'm human. He made a massive fuss about humans setting foot in his territory."

"He appears to have forgotten that little detail since I told him about what you did today."

"I didn't do anything," I insisted. "I didn't stop Jada. I barely completed the incantation and she broke through it with no trouble. We would have been just as dead if Rickards hadn't shown up."

"You saved Eeps and you slowed Jada down long enough for Rickards to get there. From where I sit, it looks like your magic saved the day." Jamie cracked one of his glorious smiles and clapped me on the shoulder. "I hate to be the one to burst your bubble, girlfriend, but it's official and you can't wriggle out of it no matter how hard you try. You're a witch, and a damn good one, too."

ABOUT WENDY MEADOWS

Wendy Meadows is a USA Today bestselling author whose stories showcase women sleuths. To date, she has published dozens of books, which include her popular Sweetfern Harbor series, Sweet Peach Bakery series, and Alaska Cozy series, to name a few. She lives in the "Granite State" with her husband, two sons, two mini pigs and a lovable Labradoodle.

Join Wendy's newsletter to stay up-to-date with new releases. As a subscriber, you'll also get BLACKVINE MANOR, the complete series, for FREE!

Join Wendy's Newsletter Here
wendymeadows.com/cozy